MESSAGE
in the BLADE

Dawn Merriman

Dedication

This book is dedicated to my wonderful husband, Kevin who always inspires me. Thank you for always supporting me. Also dedicated to Carlie Frech, Belinda Martin, and Katie Hoffman for all thier insights and encouragement.

-Dawn Merriman

Prologue

Blood pounds through me as I think of what I'll soon be doing. My hands shake on the steering wheel, small tremors of anticipation.

"Keep your cool," I tell myself.

I love this part, the knowing what's coming, the waiting for the rush that will fill me when it's done. I relish all of it, the planning, the thinking of the deed. The rush, like now, as I approach the destination where they wait for me.

They wait for my retribution.

They have no idea I am coming, but they need redeeming.

It's my calling to make them pay for their mistakes.

My calling.

I like the sound of that.

My mind drifts, as it often does, to the seven nights before this one. To the satisfaction I've gotten knowing the world is a better place thanks to me.

7

And I think of her.

I park a few blocks down the street from where tonight's job waits for me.

I know he's sleeping. I've watched him for days, learned his habits. He does his deadly business while the porch light is on. The light is off now.

He sleeps.

He waits.

I tremble with excitement.

I slip on the mask.

Now I feel whole. The mask completes me, more natural than my own skin.

Only in the mask do I feel fully alive.

I flip up the hood of my hoodie and pull the strings. The gun in the front pocket pulls the dark sweater down. The weight of it makes me feel so good, I can hardly stand it. I slip my hand into the pocket and caress the cool metal. Soon the metal will be hot.

A shiver of anticipation slides across my shoulders.

A pair of latex gloves are in my back pocket and I put them on. I wish I could touch things, touch him when he's gone. Wish my bare skin could feel the heat of the gun flash.

But I have to be careful. I know the rules.

The street is dark, the few street lights have been broken by wayward stones thrown by wayward teens.

The entire neighborhood needs redeemed.

I'm working on it.

After tonight this block will be better.

And she will notice.

I walk with purpose, my footsteps matching the beat of blood in my ears. I push past the overgrown bushes on either side of the front walk and climb the steps to the sagging porch.

I dart a look at the neighbor's house. She's not on her porch. She spends all day there, watching, complaining. She goes in promptly at 8:30.

8:30 came and went hours ago and her porch is empty. It would be easy to do her, too. But she is one of the few here that don't need me to send her on. She has no record I could find.

God will take her soon, anyway.

I can barely breathe, I'm so excited. My chest hurts and I take a few steadying breaths. I suck in the night air slowly and exhale. The mask makes a tiny whistling sound as I breathe out.

"You've got this," I say and take the gun from my hoodie pocket. Goosebumps of excitement break out down my arms, despite the warm air and the heavy hoodie.

I reach for the knob, wrap my fingers around the worn metal and turn.

The knob turns.

The door is unlocked, just as I knew it would be.

I push the door open.

For a moment, it sticks and I fear he has an inside chain.

I shove it hard and it glides into the dark of the living room.

His room is up the stairs to the right.

I take a step into the house, every sense on edge, every nerve in my body full of adrenaline.

Slowly, silently, I creep up the stairs. At the top, I turn down the hallway. His room is at the far end of the hall, at the front of the house.

I hear him snoring loudly. The sound grates on my nerves, another transgression.

I focus on my steps, place each foot carefully.

A board squeaks, loud in the silent house.

The rhythm of his snoring changes slightly, and I freeze.

I count to ten as he falls back into a deep sleep. Only then do I take another step.

I reach the bedroom door, slightly ajar. Through the crack, I can see him. He lies on his back, the moonlight on his wispy goatee.

He must be sent away.

The wood of the door is cool under my latex-covered palm. I push on the door.

Slow steps toward the bed.

He waits.

I lift the gun.

Chapter 1

GABBY

It's been six days since I gave Lucas my necklace back. Six days since I saw Nathan taken away in an ambulance and later taken back to jail. Six days since I came back to work only to find out my shop may not survive the loss of Nathan's fake clients.

It's been a crappy six days.

Each night I see the bridge explode in my dreams. I feel the barrel of Nathan's gun on my temple. Each night I wake to an empty bed, drenched in sweat.

I sit at my desk and rub my neck, missing my necklace and all it represents. Several times a day, I pray for guidance. Pray for a sign that will let us get back together. For six days, my tattoo has been curiously silent.

I look over the bills that have come in the last week. Even with Grandma Dot not charging me rent on the building, I still have utilities and other overhead to pay. Not to mention my mortgage and credit card payments. The tiny trickle of real clients I've had this week barely covers it.

I may have to look for another line of work.

I lower my forehead to the desk and for the hundredth time wonder what in the world I will do. Why did I think I could do this? Why did I let Grandma talk me into making a living with my gift?

The bell on the front door jingles and I dart upright, embarrassed to be caught with my head down.

A sandy haired man gives me an uncertain smile. "Are you Gabby McAllister?" he asks, running a fingernail across the front of the desk nervously.

"I'm Gabby. How can I help you?" I push thoughts of explosions and necklaces to the back of my mind and give him what I think is a winning smile.

I'm hoping he's a potential client, not someone who's come to see the "freak" from the news. Lacey did her best to keep me out of the story about her sister, but this town knows who I am and what I do. This man wouldn't be the first one that just wanted to see me up close.

"I understand you're a psychic," he says, working his fingernail into the wood of my desk.

"I suppose so. Is there something I can do for you?" I'm starting to think this isn't a client and am irritated by the interruption.

"Can you talk to the dead?" he asks.

I take a deep breath. I've been asked this before. "If you know about me, you know that's not exactly what I do. I get messages when I touch certain items. If I touch a dead body, I might get a vision of how and when they died, but I don't 'talk' to them."

"Right. Right." He stops digging into my desk and shoves his hands in his pockets.

"Why don't you tell me what you need and I'll tell you if I can help or not."

He stares out the front windows into the town square. "It's my uncle. He was murdered a few days ago."

This is not what I expected to hear. I lean forward in my chair, all ears now.

"Was that here in River Bend? I don't remember seeing it on the news."

I'm wondering how a murder happened and I didn't know about it.

"You wouldn't have. It was ruled a suicide."

"I see." I don't really. "So why do you think he was murdered?"

He looks me straight in the face for the first time. "Uncle Andy would never kill himself. I know he wouldn't." His voice rises with conviction.

I search his face and he believes every word he is saying. "Do you know who ruled it a suicide?"

"The first officer that showed up, Hawthorne. And then, of course, the coroner made her ruling."

I stand with a notebook, come from behind the desk and invite the man to sit on the yellow couch. I take my usual place in one of the red chairs. "Why don't we start at the beginning," I say. "And not to be indelicate, but have you been to my website and seen my fees?"

I hate the words, but the pile of bills on my desk makes me say them.

He shifts in his seat. "I have. I'll pay whatever you want if you can prove Uncle Andy did not take his own life and find the person that killed him."

"I will do my best, but as for the last part, I am not a cop. I don't catch killers. I just help the police."

13

"Whatever it takes to bring him justice."

"Okay then. Tell me everything. Let's start with your name."

"Roger Belkin." He stares at my feet as he tells his story. "That night I was supposed to meet Uncle Andy at the sports club to have a few drinks and play pool. He never showed."

I interrupt and ask his uncle's full name. "Andrew Tippins. So when he didn't show up, I drove to his house. I was pretty upset that he stood me up and wasn't answering his calls. You have to understand, he's my uncle and I love him, but he's doesn't stay on the straight and narrow. He might have a side job that he runs from home, if you know what I mean."

"Do you mean he deals drugs?"

Roger looks away, but nods. "So I was pretty upset. I thought maybe he had decided to stay home and partake with one of his clients. It has happened before, unfortunately." He digs his fingernail into the trim edge of the couch. "Anyway, when I got to his house, everything was dark. I mean everything. He usually leaves the front porch light on to let his clients know he's open for business. That light was off."

"Did you go in the house?"

"I did. I thought maybe he had partied earlier than usual and had passed out before it grew dark and that's why the house was dark. When I knocked, he didn't answer. The door was unlocked, so I let myself in."

"Is the door normally unlocked?"

"Usually. He doesn't live in the best part of town, but

he has so many people coming and going he just leaves it unlocked. He always says he doesn't have anything worth stealing anyway."

"So you went into the house," I prompt.

"I did and turned on the light. I expected to find him on the couch passed out. But the couch was empty. So I searched the house. I found him in his bed. He'd been shot in the head. The gun was still in his hand."

"That must have been awful."

Roger looks out the front window and swallows hard. I give him a moment to keep himself under control. "It was," he finally says. "So I called 911. They sent an officer over. Officer Hawthorne. This officer took one look at Uncle Andy and said it looked like suicide."

"Did they call the detectives in? Any death in a home like that is at least looked at by a detective."

"They did. Detective McAllister came. I believe he's your brother."

"Yes, he is. Detective McAllister agreed with Hawthorne that it was suicide?"

Roger looks away again but nods. "He did. The gun was in his hand, after all. Then the coroner came and she agreed."

I study the man. These memories are making his hands shake. He digs into the couch trim again.

"Roger, why did you come to me? It sounds like a clear case of suicide. I know that's not an easy thing for family to accept, but it happens more than we'd like to think."

He turns and looks me straight in the eye. "I know

Uncle Andy didn't shoot himself."

"How can you be so sure?"

"He didn't own a gun. He hated them. He did two tours in Afghanistan. When he came home, he was broken. Hence, the drugs. He had a hard rule about guns. Wouldn't even let his clients bring them to the house."

"So where did the gun come from?"

"Exactly. I know he had problems and the suicide might make sense for a man that had his issues. But I assure you, he would never use a gun. Never."

Chapter 2

LUCAS

It's been six days since Gabby gave me the necklace back. Six days since the mysterious message I heard in my head, in my heart that told me to go to Grandma Dot's farm.

Was it from God? Is that what Gabby hears?

All I know is the words were insistent in my head and I had to act on them. I told Dustin and we went.

As usual, Gabby had the situation under control already. Seeing her over Nathan's inert body, his gun in her hand shook me. Does she even need me?

I didn't stick around to find out. There was a crime scene that needed me more back at the old house.

Six days later, I wish I had stuck around. I wish I had given her the opportunity to tell me it was all a mistake.

I've checked my phone several times a day, even hovered my finger over the call button late one night. I had it in my head to call and beg for her to come back.

Something held my finger.

The next day, I went fishing at Harper Lake. It felt good to get out of River Bend for the day. Just me and the water and my fishing pole.

If she doesn't want me, I don't want her.

Near the water, I almost believed it.

I had missed an apparent suicide case on my day off, but Dustin had handled it fine without me. He had the new officer Hawthorne at the scene. I'd read the report and it all looked tidy. Coroner Gomez had made her ruling. Another suicide on the south side of town.

So why do I find myself reading the report again?

Nothing in the papers gives me a reason to think there was foul play. I flip the file closed on my desk and look at the empty desk facing mine. Dustin is around somewhere and I could ask him about it. I could, but I won't. He was at the scene and made his determination. I will not question his judgment.

But I can ask the other officer that responded.

I step out of our office and into the bullpen. I scan the blue shirts that are present and find the tight bun of auburn hair that I seek.

Officer Kalissta Hawthorne.

I call her name and she turns in surprise. When she sees it's me calling to her, she beams a smile.

"Can I help you, Detective Hartley?" she says as she approaches.

"Will you come into my office a moment?"

"Of course," she answers with enthusiasm. "Whatever you need."

She runs a hand over her hair, smoothing her bun.

Once in the semi-privacy of our office, I close the door. She stands stiff, almost at attention, waiting.

"Did I do something wrong?" the young officer asks.

"No, nothing like that. I just wanted to ask about a case

you were recently part of. The Andrew Tippins suicide."

She relaxes, "Oh. Okay. What do you want to know?"

What did I want to know? I suddenly feel foolish for bringing her in like this. She did her job, it is not my place to question her. She looks at me with large brown eyes a few shades darker than her auburn hair.

"Was there anything, I don't know, off about the scene?"

She tips her head in consideration. The movement combined with her wide eyes makes her look like an adorable puppy. "Nothing I can think of. The gun was in the man's hand so it was pretty cut and dried. Detective McAllister seemed to agree and so did Coroner Gomez." Those large eyes now narrow in question. "Why do you ask?"

"It's probably nothing," I say, feeling ridiculous. "Thank you for coming in."

I open the door to let her leave, then think of one last question.

"You work the south side beat, don't you?"

"Yes." The large eyes again.

I bite my lip, not sure how to word my question. "Has there been an unusual number of suicides in that area lately?"

She looks confused. "I don't know if I'd say an unusual number. That part of town is rough, people tend to do drastic things in neighborhoods like that."

I think back over the last months. "I can think of seven suicides in recent months. Not just on the south side, but five of them were in that area."

She tips her head again. "What are you asking me?"

I rub my buzz cut in agitation. "I'm not sure. Look, forget I asked."

She smiles widely. "It's no problem." She tips her head and looks up slightly through her long lashes. "You can ask me anything you need."

She then turns on her heel and leaves the office.

If I didn't know better, I'd think Kalissta Hawthorne was flirting with me.

Dustin comes down the hall and sees Hawthorne. "What's up?"

I don't want him to know I'm questioning one of his cases, so I say, "Nothing."

He looks at the retreating officer and back to me, then shakes his head and makes a sound of disgust.

"It's not like that," I say defensively.

"Hey, your personal life is not my business." He takes his seat.

"I don't have a personal life. Thanks to your sister." I try to keep the anger from my voice and manage it just barely. Dustin is my partner and my best friend. But it's a bit awkward being around my ex's brother all the time.

He spreads his hands wide, "Don't blame me for Gabby's erratic behavior. We both know she does what she wants. Or what she feels she needs to do." He softens and leans forward. "So she hasn't called yet?"

"Nope." I flop into my chair and push the Andrew Tippins file away. I'm looking for something that isn't there.

I pull out my phone and check it. There's nothing there

either.

I shove the phone back in my pocket, irritated that I even care.

Chief Simmons ducks his head into the office door. "Hey, Detectives. We just got a call from the area of that suicide earlier. Someone is breaking into the Tippins house."

"Why do you need us to go?" I ask. "Sounds like patrol can handle it."

Simmons's face grows red. "It's Gabby."

"Crap on a cracker," I say before I can catch myself. I have picked up the expression from her. I hate that the words escaped my lips.

Chapter 3

GABBY

I sit back in my chair and think about what he just said. "This sounds intriguing," I tell Roger Belkin, "But I don't know what you want me to do about it. If the coroner has already ruled, there is little that will change her ruling."

"Even if you see something different? She won't change it for you?"

I make a sound of disbelief before I can stop myself. "Sorry. Me and Gomez don't really see eye to eye."

"I thought you had an in with the police. Your brother? You've done it before."

"I have been involved in a few cases, that's true. Look I don't have a problem going to the house and seeing what I might see, but I want you to be prepared. We might not be able to do anything with whatever information we find."

Roger rubs the edge of the couch in thought, then looks up. "That will have to do. It's more than I can accomplish by myself."

I stand and he follows. "Let's go then. Do you have a key to the house?"

"I don't. I locked the door when I left, but I gave the key to my mom, his sister. I didn't think I'd need it."

"Can we get it from her?"

"She's at work right now. A doctor at the hospital. We can't bother her." He sounds truly disappointed.

So am I. I'm ready for anything that will take my mind off of Lucas.

"Well, we'll figure it out when we get there. What's the address?"

Roger excitedly tells me where the house is. "Thank you," he says, reaching to shake my hand. He sees the gloves I always wear and thinks better of it, and drops his hand.

"I'll meet you there," I say and show him to the door.

It doesn't take long to reach the address, but I don't often come to this part of town. A few people are out walking around and I think about all the customers of Andrew Tippins that will now have to find a new place to get their fix. Are the men out on the sidewalk customers?

I park behind Roger, shove my purse under the front seat and lock the doors of my gray Charger. A man across the road watches me with interest. When I meet his eyes, he walks on.

Next door to Andy's house, a rail-thin woman watches us from her seat on the sagging front porch. I meet her eyes and expect her to look away, too. But she just purses her lips and shakes her head.

"Friendly neighborhood," I say to Roger as we walk up the cracked concrete sidewalk.

"I know." He sounds almost apologetic. "I never liked Uncle Andy living way down here, but he didn't seem to mind it."

We push past overgrown bushes and climb the steps to a porch that has seen better days. Paint peels from the railing, showing several layers beneath of the different colors of the porch through the years.

I'm careful not to touch the railing, thinking of all the hands that have also touched it. I suddenly feel like this might not be a good idea. A house like this has seen some history. I can feel it surrounding me, a slight sizzle in the air. I tuck my hands into my armpits.

"Try the door," I say.

Roger wiggles the handle, but it is locked.

"Crap on a cracker. I'd hoped we'd get lucky."

I feel eyes on my back and turn to see the old woman next door has left her chair. She stands at the side of her porch, openly staring at us.

"Looks like we'll have to use the window," Roger says. The large front window is as worn out as the porch. It doesn't take him long to remove the screen and shimmy it up.

"Ready?" he asks, then ducks inside. With a last look at the woman next door staring at me, I climb in, too.

The house is surprisingly clean but outdated. I've never been in a drug dealer's house before and didn't know what to expect. The carpet is worn, but vacuumed. A flowered couch is against the far wall, facing a TV next to the window we climbed through. A faded blue recliner sits in the corner. Roger looks around, his face pinched.

"Strange, for a moment I forgot that Uncle Andy would not be sitting in his usual chair."

"I'm so sorry for your loss," I offer sincerely. "This must be hard on you."

He takes a deep breath. "Yeah. He and I were very close. My dad wasn't around much and my mom never remarried. Andy kind of stepped in. He had his faults, but he loved me," he says wistfully.

"I'm sure he did," I say quietly. "Mind if I look around?"

Roger comes back to the present. "Of course. Help yourself to anything that might be useful."

"I think I should start with where you found him."

He leads me up the steps to a small bedroom in the front of the house. The bed sheets have been removed. The mattress is stained in several places, with a large stain near the head of the bed. I can tell its blood.

I approach the stain and peel off my gloves. I look to Roger. "Do you mind stepping out of the room? This is kind of a personal thing I do."

"No problem. However it works."

He steps into the hall and I hold my hand above the stain. "Lord, let me see what I need to see," I say my usual prayer. I take a deep breath, close my eyes and drop my hand.

Peaceful sleep. Resting. A moment of surprise.

There is nothing else. I open my eyes and blink several times to clear my mind. There has to be something. Of course, if he was asleep when he was shot, there wouldn't be much to see.

I wish I had Lacey with me so we could combine our powers, but I know she wouldn't come if I asked her.

I can manage on my own.

I pray again, really concentrate and touch the stain.

I get the same peaceful sense, the same short moment of surprise. The man died instantly. I search for a detail, anything that might help the investigation.

Andy only saw the shooter's face for a split second. I focus on that second. The face is blurry, white, unnaturally white.

I pull my hand away and gasp for air. I feel like I've been punched in the gut from the effort of playing the vision over and over.

Roger hears me gasping and comes back into the room. "Are you okay?"

"I'm fine. Sometimes the visions just knock the wind out of me." I pull my gloves back on while I catch my breath.

"Did you see anything? Did he shoot himself?"

I look him in the eye. "He did not shoot himself. He was shot in his sleep. I couldn't get a look at the killer really. A white face. That's all I could see, all he saw in that split second."

Roger covers his mouth with his hand. "I knew it," he says triumphantly. "We have to call the cops, we need to tell your brother."

I shake my head. "It won't do any good. Especially if the news comes from me. I told you not to get your hopes up."

"But I can't just let the killer get away with this," he says miserably.

I look at the floor. I feel bad for the man, but I don't

know what else I can do.

"I'm sorry. There's no way the coroner will get involved just on what I see."

"So that's it?"

"You can go to Dustin if you want. Maybe you'll get lucky. I don't know. I'm not really on the best terms with the department right now."

He looks at the stain on the mattress and at my hands. "So you really saw something? You saw him get killed?"

"I did," I say gravely.

"That must be hard on you. To see people die."

I'm surprised at his kindness. Most don't think about what a toll seeing murder takes on me. Not only physically, but emotionally. "It is. But I manage."

He leads the way back downstairs. I follow him into the front room.

"Well, I guess you've done all you can," he says awkwardly. "Um, how do I pay you?"

I hate this part. I truly hate it.

But a girl's got to eat.

"I like cash if you have it."

He reaches into his pocket and hands me a wad of bills. "I got this before I came. I knew you'd help me."

I quickly slide the bills into my pocket without insulting him by counting it out.

We leave the house through the front door and not the window.

We're pushing past the overgrown bushes when a whoop whoop of a cop car sounds in front of the house.

"Gabby, what in the world are you doing now?" my

brother barks.

A few steps behind him, looking like he'd rather be anywhere other than near me, is the man I still love. My heart tears anew when I see Lucas.

"I'm on a job," I say, wishing Lucas would lift his eyes from the road and look at me.

Dustin scoffs. "A job? And this job just happens to be where a man died a few days ago?"

Roger comes to my defense, "I hired her to look into my uncle's death. I brought her here."

"And broke into the house? The neighbor called about two suspicious people climbing through the window. Said one was that psychic lady."

I look over my shoulder at the house next door. The old lady is watching, her arms crossed and her face full of satisfaction.

She smiles at me, a creepy, evil smile of dislike. The toothless grin is unsettling and I turn back to the men.

"We didn't exactly break in. Roger's mom has the key and we couldn't get it from her. Technically the house belongs to the family now. Besides, it's not a crime scene."

Dustin knows I'm right and his shoulders slump. Lucas still has not raised his eyes. He scans the now empty sidewalks, but won't look at me.

I can't blame him.

"Gabby, for God's sake," Dustin exclaims.

"Exactly. God's," I say. "Aren't you even curious about what I saw?"

He looks to Lucas for support but doesn't get it.

29

"What?"

"Andrew Tippins didn't shoot himself. He was murdered in his sleep."

"I knew it," Lucas says. He meets my eyes for a split second, long enough for tingles to run down my spine, then drops his eyes to the road.

Dustin looks from me to Lucas. "What are we supposed to do with this information now?" he says in disbelief.

"Figure out who killed Uncle Andy," Roger says.

Chapter 4

GABBY

Dustin blows air in exasperation, looks at me sideways, and then asks, "You sure about this?"

I raise my eyebrows and give him a scathing look. "Really?"

"It's just if I'm going to go against Gomez, I need something more than a vision from you. She won't believe it no matter what. Tell me everything you saw."

"There wasn't a lot to see. Andy was sleeping when he was woken up by someone nearby. He saw the person for a split second. Then he was gone."

"Did you get a look at the person, something we can use?"

I shake my head a little and say, "Just a white face." I think through the vision again. "Not exactly a face, it was kind of blurry."

"So a white male?"

"I didn't say male, I can't tell. And the face was white, but I'm not sure the person was. They were dressed all in black, even gloves. I didn't see skin. Just the white where a face should be. A mask maybe?"

"Dressed in black with a mask," Lucas says

sarcastically. "That's a big help."

"I don't get to choose what the visions show," I say defensively, my voice shaking a little.

"Of course not. You just believe whatever the vision says," Lucas says angrily. We both know we're talking about how I broke up with him, not about Andy's murder.

"I didn't ask for this," I say, my anger growing.

"But you didn't say no. You didn't fight it."

"I had no choice."

Lucas finally looks me in the eye. "Yes, you did have a choice. We all have a choice. You made yours."

We hold eyes a moment and I lose myself in the blue of his. I want to throw myself at his feet, tell him I'm sorry. I almost give in.

Not yet.

Traitorous tattoo.

I clamp my hand over the tingle in my arm. Lucas sees the action and makes a sound of disgust. "See? A choice." He throws his hands up and stalks away and climbs into the cruiser.

Dustin clears his throat and I'm suddenly reminded that I'm standing on the cracked sidewalk in front of the house where Andy was murdered. Roger is looking at me in confusion.

"I'm sorry," I mumble. "That wasn't about the case."

"Yeah, I kind of picked up on that," he says gently.

"You're even stupider than I thought, psychic lady," the old woman from the front porch yells across the yard. "If I had a man like that I'd never let him walk away."

I look over my shoulder at the woman, all kinds of

sharp retorts ready on my tongue, when I feel Dustin's hand on my arm.

"Don't. Just focus on the case."

I meet his eyes and see comfort there. If we were anywhere else, I might take refuge in a brotherly hug. Now is not the time.

"So, what's our next step?" I ask.

"Our," he motions to Lucas in the cruiser, "Next step is to try to get the case reopened." He looks to Roger. "I will do all I can, but I can't promise anything."

Roger nods. "Gabby explained all that to me. I'm just glad you are looking into it. It will clear Uncle Andy's name. Everyone will know he did not shoot himself." He swallows hard, his Adam's apple bobbing.

Dustin shakes Roger's hand. "I'll be in touch."

"Thank you, Detective McAllister." Roger shakes Dustin's hand vigorously and then reaches for my hand. No one ever shakes hands with me.

To my surprise, he takes my gloved hand in both of his. "You're amazing. I can't thank you enough." He pumps my hand a few times then lets go.

"If you need anything else, let me know," I say as he walks away.

"I'll do that." He waves and climbs into his car. After he's gone, Dustin and I stand alone on the sidewalk.

"You doing okay?" he asks in unusual kindness.

"Okay, I guess." I toe a crack in the concrete. "Getting by. Have you heard anything about Nathan?"

"Not since they moved him to that new jail. The guard he bribed to escape was found a few days ago and has been booked. I don't know anything else."

"Hmm," I say, beginning to feel awkward.

"Look," he starts. "I know I'm not an expert on relationships, but this thing with you and Lucas-."

I raise my eyes to his. "Is none of your business."

"In a way, it is my business. He's my best friend and my partner. You're my sister. I love you both and you love each other. Whatever this is, whatever you feel you need to do, just hurry. You two have a good thing. I'd hate for you to lose it. Relationships are complicated enough."

I get the feeling he's talking about him and Alexis, that there's been trouble at home. I know Alexis has been going to Alcoholics Anonymous meetings for the last few months and keeping it secret from Dustin. I want to tell him, but I promised Alexis I wouldn't.

"I know you're trying to help and I appreciate it. If I understood this, I would tell you."

Lucas bumps the horn in the cruiser, the noise makes me jump.

"Looks like I better go," Dustin says. He suddenly puts his arm around my shoulders and pulls me against his chest. His chest is hard with his vest, but I allow myself to enjoy the moment of love.

"Get going. You have a case to solve," I say when he releases me, feeling awkward at the affection.

"Hang in there," he says, then crosses the road and climbs into the cruiser.

I watch the only two men I love drive away.

I feel the old woman watching me, judging me.

"Shut up," I say under my breath and climb into my

Charger.

I don't have any clients for the rest of the day. Sitting at the shop, worrying, or going home to an empty house, both fill me with dread. Instead, I go to Grandma Dot's. The beauty shop is open and there's bound to be a distraction there. Plus, Mom has been working at the shop a few days a week. Today is one of her work days.

I run my fingers through my long, dark, curls and they tangle in the mop of hair. Maybe I need a change. Maybe a haircut will do me good.

I drive, my mind bouncing between thoughts of Andy Tippins's murder and haircuts. I want to think of anything other than the confrontation with Lucas and how handsome he looks in his uniform.

"Why, God?" I say out loud. "Why keep us apart?"

If I really expected an answer, I'm disappointed.

I park next to the barn, take note that the door is shut tight, and make my way up the steps to the back door when I reach Grandma Dot's. The early May sunshine is warm on my face, the soft breeze is like an embrace. A robin lands on the railing of the porch and cocks its head at me.

I look at the bird, one of God's creatures, and revel in the wonder of nature. The bird stares back, twitching its head back and forth.

"Hi, there," I say to it.

It continues to stare another moment, then flies away. The small exchange fills me with peace, with faith. God is watching over me. I don't need to understand anything else.

With new vigor, I enter the kitchen. Through the sliding doors that separate the beauty shop from the rest of the house, I hear Grandma saying something and Mom laughing in response.

Yes, my personal life may be a mess and there's a new murderer in River Bend, but this moment here is perfect.

I place my hand on the sliding doors, ready to enter the beauty shop when I hear another familiar voice.

My new-found sister, Lacey Aniston.

I slide the doors open and walk into a scene I never thought I'd see. Lacey is in Grandma Dot's chair, foil papers in her hair. In all my life, Lacey has never had her hair done by Grandma Dot. I stare at her reflection in the mirror. She's the first one to see me.

"Gabby," she says with sincere excitement. Even after everything we've been through, I'm not used to being on friendly terms with her. Years of being enemies, of being the butt of her jokes in high school, an object of ridicule on her TV newscasts as adults, make this new relationship seem weird. Nice, but still weird.

"Hey, Lacey," I say with a little awkward wave. "Looks like you're in good hands."

I had planned on getting my own hair cut, but quickly decide against it. We may be sisters, but getting our hair done together is a little too much for me just yet.

"I was overdue for a color, and I thought, why haven't I ever gone to Dot's?"

Because she hated my family up until a week or two ago. But I don't say that.

"She has such lovely hair," Grandma chimes in, and

Lacey beams.

"What brings you here?" Mom says from the wash sink where she is rinsing out color bottles. There are no other customers in the shop besides Lacey. I hesitate and dart my eyes to hers in the mirror.

"Spill it. I can tell something is on your mind. Off the record," Lacey says with a wide smile.

"What's said in the beauty shop stays in the beauty shop," Grandma says.

"I had a new client this morning," I start. "His uncle was killed. It had been ruled as a suicide, but he was sure it wasn't."

"How awful," Mom says.

I tell them about going to the house and what I saw. Lacey listens with interest, especially to the part about touching the stain.

I leave out the part about Lucas getting upset with me and the small hug Dustin gave me.

"So they're going to reopen the case?" Lacey asks.

"Going to try. You cannot put this on TV. You can't tell anyone what I saw."

"I won't." She sounds insulted that I'd even mention it. "I promise. At least, not until there's something official to report."

Grandma finishes the last foil on Lacey's highlight and puts the color dish and brush in the sink for Mom to wash.

"The only question that matters is what are you going to do about it?" Grandma asks me.

The question catches me off guard. "What do you mean? I already did what I was hired to do."

All three women look at me with various expressions of disbelief. "You're going to stay out of the case?" Grandma asks, obviously not believing me.

"What do you want me to do? I'm not a cop."

"Never stopped you before," she points out.

I don't want to talk about it, so I change the subject. "How's Aubry? Is she recovered from her ordeal?"

"She's getting by. She's taking Brent's death pretty hard. Blames herself since the killers were after her and he was in the way."

"I heard his service was lovely," Grandma says. "So many people. His cousin was in here the day after and she told me all about it."

"It was a nice service. Just so sad," Lacey says and bows her foil-covered head.

The mood in the shop is sober and Grandma changes the subject. "You all heard about Mrs. Mott's party tomorrow, right? You are all invited."

I'd honestly forgotten about it, but I say that I remember.

"She wants everyone to meet her new boyfriend, Derek. I've met him. He's a retired detective, recently moved here to River Bend. You'd like him, Gabriella."

"Why's that?"

"I don't know. He's nice. He has lots of interesting stories about his days on the force." Grandma shrugs and checks Lacey's foils.

"I think I've had my fill of detectives for a while. Retired old guys, or not."

"He's not that old. Younger than Pauline and me."

"That's old," I tease.

"You're impossible. Will you come? Pauline will be hurt if you don't."

I don't want to go, but I can't let Mrs. Mott down. "I'll be there."

"It's at his place out on that private lake community. What's it called again?"

"Willow Shores," Mom offers. "I've wanted to go see that place. The lake is man-made and there are only a few houses on it. That abandoned mansion is on one end of the lake. Sounds so interesting."

"Not sure how a retired detective has the money for such a place, but it's none of my business," Grandma says.

"Uh-huh," I say. "None of your business, so keep it that way."

"What? You calling me nosey?"

"I'm calling you overly concerned."

"That's right. Concerned."

"Want to come with me?" Lacey asks. "We can drive together."

I haven't heard from Lacey in the week since our adventure, and I'm not sure what this sudden urge to be close is about. She seems genuine, though. "Okay. But I'm driving."

She smiles and then jumps. She reaches for her pocket and takes out her cell phone. It buzzes in her hand. "Sorry, it's work," she says and takes the call.

After a moment of listening, she says, "I understand. Text me the address and I'll be there as soon as I can." She hangs up the phone and looks at our three curious faces.

"Gabby, you want to come to a story with me?" she asks.

I'm surprised to be invited, but agree to go before I even think about it. "Why take me along?"

"There's another death on the south side of town. Our source say it's another suicide. There's been a rash of suicides in town the last few weeks. That's what they want me to do the story on."

"Another suicide?" Mom asks. "How sad that so many people have been driven to that decision."

"Unless it's not suicide," I point out. "Just like Roger's uncle this morning."

"There's been about eight that I know of," Lacey says.

"And if they are not all self-inflicted, that means we have a murderer on the loose."

"Worse than that," I say soberly. "We have a serial killer."

The room goes silent.

After a shocked moment, Grandma starts pulling the foils from Lacey's hair. "You two need to get there and start looking into this. Don't let that coroner rule this one wrong," she says to me.

I don't know how I can stop Gomez from doing what she wants, but I promise to try.

Chapter 5

GABBY

As I follow Lacey's car to the scene, I brace myself for seeing Lucas twice on the same day. I toy with the idea of turning around, of letting Dustin take care of the new threat, but I keep driving. If there really is a serial killer in River Bend, one staging the murders to look like suicides, then it will take all of us to stop them.

When we arrive at the scene, I'm surprised at how close we are to Andy Tippins's house. Only a few blocks away. This neighborhood is even more run-down than his was. Definitely not the shiniest part of River Bend.

There are only two police cars on the scene when we arrive. One I recognize as the cruiser Lucas and Dustin were in earlier, at least it has the same number. I don't suppose I'll get lucky enough to do whatever I need to without seeing them. The other cruiser, I assume belongs to the responding officer. I hope I'll get extra lucky and it's officer Patterson. He won't turn me away on sight.

No luck. A pretty female officer with her hair in a neat auburn bun walks out the door of the ramshackle house with the crooked blue shutters. I recognize her as one of the new recruits this spring, but we've never met. I hope to win her over. I could use another ally like Patterson.

41

I park on the street behind Lacey who parks behind the news van already here and waiting for her. She introduces me to her cameraman, Nick. I've seen him with her many times, but have never wanted to know his name. He's always been the anonymous man trying to get a close-up of my face and tape my reaction as Lacey shames me on film.

Nick seems confused as to why Lacey and I are suddenly so chummy, but doesn't ask questions. He fills her in on what he's been told about the scene so far.

"A white female, twenty-four years old. Her name is Shelly Parker," Nick says. "Looks like she took a bottle of pills. Honestly, I don't see why we are here."

"We'll see," Lacey says. "Have the detectives come out yet?"

"No. They have that officer guarding the door. She gave me a dirty look when I pulled up but hasn't chased me away yet."

"This is a public road, she can't make us leave," Lacey says opening her purse and taking out a tube of lipstick. She uses the side view mirror of the van to apply the lipstick. As she rubs her lips together, she looks at me, all business.

"You think you can go in there and get a statement. Or better yet, convince Lucas or Dustin to come talk to us?"

I open my un-lipsticked mouth in surprise. "They won't let me in."

"You don't know that. Charm that boyfriend of yours."

"We broke up, remember."

Her cheeks turn a pretty shade of pink. "Oh, yeah.

Sorry. I forgot. I was hoping you'd get us a way in. Maybe this is a bad idea," she says dismissively. This is more like the Lacey I'm used to.

"I'm here now," I say. "I'll go see what I can find out. Maybe that officer on guard is a fan."

Nick makes a small laughing sound, then quickly shuts up when Lacey smacks his arm. "You never know."

I feel eyes from the surrounding houses on me as I make my way up the walk. The neighborhood has seen better decades and looks deserted now that the police are here, but I sense all the curious lookers at windows down the block.

The officer at the door watches me with a guarded expression. I try for bravado and say, "Hi, thanks for guarding the scene," and try to walk past her like I am expected inside.

She doesn't fall for the ruse and steps in front of me. "You can't go in there, Ms. McAllister."

I check her name tag and say, "Look, Officer Hawthorne, I need to see the scene here. Dustin and Lucas are expecting me." I try to make my way around her, but she sidesteps in front of me again.

"I doubt your brother or your ex want to see you right now. They're on a case."

I wonder how she knows that Lucas and I are no longer together. Is our personal life news all over town?

"You don't know that. Please step aside, Officer Hawthorne." I use my most authoritative voice.

She doesn't fall for this either, and not so subtly rests her hand on the gun at her hip. "Why don't you go back to your friend with the news van and leave us to do the actual work." I'm surprised at the vicious tone of her words. For a woman I've never met, she sure doesn't like me.

"Kalissta, is that the coroner you're talking to?" Lucas suddenly says, appearing in the doorway of the small house. "Oh no," he groans when he sees me. "Dustin. Your sister is here."

Dismissed, I stand on the weedy front walk as Dustin comes to the door. This morning he was unusually friendly. Now, he's fuming.

"You can't be serious," he says, looking past me to the news van. Lacey is standing with Nick, who has his camera facing us. "You brought the press."

"Actually, she brought me. Dustin, look. Doesn't it seem strange that you have yet another suicide in town? I don't think this girl, Shelly, did this to herself."

Kalissta snorts in derision. "Why don't you let the detectives decide that? They don't need your help."

I wish Lucas would come back outside and stand up for me. But the doorway remains empty. Dustin runs a hand over his hair in agitation. "She's right. We've got this. You better get out of here before Gomez comes and arrests you like she's threatened to do."

"Arrest me for helping?"

"For interfering with police work," Kalissta Hawthorne interjects.

"I don't need you interfering in *my* work," I snap at her.

"Your work is a joke," she says, taking a step toward

me.

"That's enough," Lucas says decisively from the doorway. "Officer Hawthorne, stand down. Gabby, please leave. Your concern about Shelly Parker has been noted."

Kalissta goes to stand beside Lucas, a little too close for my taste. She smiles in victory. I clench my gloved hands into fists at my side, wanting to smack that smile from her face.

"Really, Gabby," Dustin says. "I promise we'll look into all the angles. We always do. This poor soul was a prostitute and into meth as well as pills. We've seen her in and out of jail many times. She had a hard life. It's unfortunate that she may have chosen pills as a way to escape this."

"What if she didn't? What if this is like the Andy Tippins case?"

"The Tippins case is closed," Officer Hawthorne chimes in. I shoot her a deadly glance.

"Only for now," I say.

"Go home, Gabby," she says. I take a step towards her, at the last edge of my patience with the woman. She steps forward, too. Lucas puts a hand on her shoulder to hold her back. The sight of his hand on her makes my irritation turn to rage.

Dustin sees the change and steps in front of me just in time to stop me from rushing her. "Stop this. Don't embarrass us both," he whispers in my ear.

This halts me in my tracks. I relax and step away from the three uniforms. "You promise not to rush to a manner of death?"

"I'll do what I can," Dustin says. "Now please, let us get back to work."

I scan their faces. Lucas is looking at the ground like he can't even stand to see me. Hawthorne is beaming like she won. Dustin seems ashamed.

I turn from them and walk towards my car.

I'm conscious of Nick's camera and that it taped the entire shameful situation. Trusting that Lacey won't put the video on the news, I climb into my Charger. It roars to life. I see a curtain flutter in the nearest house. Someone's been watching me all the way to my car.

I put the Charger in drive and speed away. I'm driving too fast, but I don't care. Maybe Officer Hawthorne will come give me a ticket.

I'd like to see her try.

Chapter 6

LUCAS

Seeing Gabby twice in one day is almost too much. Watching her lose her temper with Officer Hawthorne stirs something in me. I don't like to see her upset. Especially when I think she's right.

Once inside the front room of the small, ramshackle house, alone with Dustin, I say as much. "You know she's right. There has been an unusual number of suicides lately. Not to mention accidental deaths, too now that I think about it."

Dustin takes a deep breath, "I know. I just don't want her marching in here and telling us what to do. We have to find a better way for her to be involved. This isn't working."

I'm surprised at his agreement, was braced for the opposite.

"What are you thinking?"

He sighs again. "I have no idea. Let's worry about Shelly Parker for now and hope the rest works its way out."

We walk down the short hall to the bedroom where a concerned friend found the body of Shelly Parker. The young woman looks much older than her years. Her arms are rail thin, several bracelets on each wrist. Her face is marred with a few sores, and her hair is straggly and spread across the pillow. She looks like she's sleeping.

I feel sorry for the woman who had such a hard time. Last time we had contact with her, she'd vowed to get her life in order. I'd have to check, but it seems like at least six months since she'd been picked up for prostitution.

Judging by the paraphernalia near the bed, she hadn't given up the meth. An empty bottle of Hydrocodone is on the bed next to her. There's a half-full glass of water on the nightstand.

"Hmm," I mumble, looking at the glass.

"What?" Dustin asks.

"The glass. It's sitting neatly in place, but the pill bottle is on the bed."

"So? She put the glass down out of habit."

"And dropped the bottle?" I'm not sure why the glass is bothering me, but something just doesn't seem right.

"It's not like the pills killed her instantly. It takes time for them to kick in."

"Yeah, I guess you're right." I let it go, but my eyes are drawn back to the glass as we complete our investigation.

"Plus, it's half-full," I say a few moments later, unable to drop the subject.

Dustin turns and faces me directly. "What are you getting at? So she didn't finish the water. So what?"

"Do you ever take pills and not finish the glass?"

"Yeah, sometimes."

"I don't. I always down the rest of the water."

"So she didn't."

"But that many pills would take a lot of water. If she took them."

He walks over and takes a closer look at the glass. "I don't get it. What are you saying?"

"I'm not sure. But if someone forced the pills into her mouth and then forced her to drink the water to swallow them. It wouldn't take the whole glass. Maybe he just gave her enough to get the pills down, then sat the glass here on the nightstand."

Dustin thinks a moment. "I see your point. You think Gabby's onto something with this murderer in town scenario."

"I hate to admit it, but this is two dead bodies that may not actually be suicides. Who knows how many more there could be."

"But how do we know Shelly Parker didn't just down the pills herself?" He points to the needles strewn next to the water glass. "This will make you do crazy things."

I hear Hawthorne greeting someone outside the door. Gomez is here.

"There's only one way to know." I quickly slide one of Shelly's many bracelets off her unnaturally thin wrist.

"You can't take that," Dustin whispers.

"We need to take something to Gabby." I slide the bracelet into my pocket just as Gomez comes down the hall.

"Good afternoon, Detectives," she says, her inflection on detectives sounding sarcastic.

I brace myself to deal with the caustic woman and pat my pocket.

"Coroner Gomez," Dustin and I say at the same time.

"Looks like we have another one," she says. "I understand this one is a prostitute and a meth head?"

"This one," I say pointedly, "Is a young woman who's had a rough time."

Gomez flips her wrist, blowing me off. "Same thing."

I grit my teeth to keep a sharp retort off my tongue and leave the small bedroom that is cramped with the three of us in there.

The breeze outside feels sweet after the stuffy rooms of Shelly's house.

"Lucas, done so soon?" Hawthorne asks. There's a barely discernable purr to her voice. One I've been trying to ignore the last few days.

"It's Detective Hartley," I say in a way I hope will crush her hopes but not upset her.

Her cheeks turn pink and she straightens her shoulders. "Yes, of course, Detective." She points to a small man lurking on the sidewalk. "That man would like to speak with you or Detective McAllister."

"I'll take it." I stride across the weedy yard, feeling Hawthorne's eyes following me. Poor thing, I know she has a crush on me, but regardless of Gabby and my current status, I'm not interested.

The man on the sidewalk looks decidedly uncomfortable as I approach. He shoves his hands deep into the cut off shorts he's wearing and shuffles his bare feet on the sidewalk.

"Are you a detective?"

"I am. My officer said you wanted to talk to me."

"I saw him," the man says.

He has my full attention now. "You saw who?"

"The man who killed Shelly. She'd never take all the pills like I heard they said she did."

"Tell me about the man you saw."

"Last night. Real late. I was out here smoking," he looks down quickly, "A cigarette. Smoking a cigarette on the porch."

"It's okay. I don't care what you were smoking. Just tell me what you saw."

"It was late, like I said. Everything around was quiet. I heard Shelly's door shut. I looked because I thought it was odd. Shelly isn't out late like that anymore. She works mornings down at the Superstore now. A cashier, I think."

"The man?" I try to get the neighbor back on track.

"Right, anyway, I heard her front door and I looked. A man wearing all black was coming down the walk, really fast. He went that way and a moment later I saw tail lights driving away."

"Did you see the vehicle."

"No, just the lights. It was a car, though. Not a truck or SUV or anything."

"Did you see anything else? His face maybe?"

He looks at the sidewalk again, "His face? That's just it, that's why I paid attention."

"What do you mean?"

"He didn't have a face. It was white, blank white. I think it was a mask."

A shiver goes down my spine. A blank white face like Gabby saw at Andrew Tippins's.

We have a killer in town.

I tell the man to hang around and we'll be back to take an official statement, then go back to Shelly's house to find Dustin and Gomez.

I explain what the man saw. Gomez seems unimpressed.

"Probably some john that she invited back to her house and was into kinky stuff," she says.

I can't tell her that Gabby saw the same masked face this morning. "The neighbor said she was working at the Superstore now. We haven't picked her up for months. I don't think she was into that line of work anymore," I say.

"That you know of," Gomez challenges.

"Just keep the case open for a few days. Let us look into the possibility that the man had something to do with it." I want to tell her about the water glass and my thoughts on it, but I don't think she'll understand.

She looks from me to Dustin then back to me. "You serious about this, Hartley?"

I nod.

"And you, McAllister? You in agreement that this may be foul play?"

"Based on the neighbor's statement, it needs further investigation."

She fingers the long french braid hanging over her shoulder, thinking. "Two days," she finally says. "You have two days until I make my ruling."

I open my mouth to argue. Two days isn't long enough to do a thorough investigation and she knows it.

Dustin's hand on my arm keeps my mouth shut.

"Thank you, Coroner Gomez," he says in his most solicitous tone. "While we are discussing this topic, we have serious doubts about the Andrew Tippins case, too."

She flips the braid over her shoulder. "That case was closed days ago. You were the detective on scene and made the report."

"I know that," Dustin says, "But I've been thinking on it and I feel it needs looked at more closely."

Gomez takes a step towards us, too close in the crowded room. "I heard about your sister breaking into that Tippins house this morning. Your request wouldn't have anything to do with her, would it?"

Dustin raises his chin, "We owe it to Andrew Tippins to do our job the best we can."

"Andrew Tippins was a drug dealer. That neighborhood is better off without him."

"He was also a veteran and a beloved uncle. His nephew has asked us to look into it," I say, doing all I can to stay civil.

Gomez steps back. "Fine. I'll change my ruling to undetermined. But you still only have two days. We have actual cases that need your attention. We can't afford for you to go chasing crazy hunches."

We take our victory as it comes, mumble thank yous, and duck out of the scene.

Two days.

I pat the bracelet in my pocket.

I need all the info I can get. If that means seeing Gabby again, then that's what I'll do.

My heart flutters a little at the thought.

Chapter 7

GABBY

I need to run. I need to put in my earbuds and pound the trail at the park.

First I need my running shoes.

I let myself in the front door, pet Chester, and pull off my cut-off shorts. I haven't gone running in quite some time, but look forward to pushing myself, to the music, to the high that is sure to follow.

I find my running clothes at the bottom of a drawer and dig my shoes out of the closet. After pulling my hair into a high ponytail, I'm ready. I let myself out again and bounce down the front steps.

Only then do I see my neighbor and previous boyfriend, Preston, getting out of his car in his driveway.

"Crap on a cracker," I mutter and debate going back inside until he is in his house. I've managed to only talk to him a few times since we broke up months ago. After having to see Lucas twice today, I'm not up for more ex drama.

Preston sees me, stops in his driveway, and waves a friendly hello.

"I see you're going running," he says as he crosses the property line.

I feel self-conscious in my tight running pants and tank top. I resist the urge to cross my arms over my chest, and I put on a smile.

"I'm headed to the park. I haven't been keeping up with my running routine. Plus, I want to check out the repairs they are making to the bridge."

"The one you blew up," he teases.

"I didn't blow it up. Nathan did," I say a bit defensively. I think of the nightmares of the bridge blowing up. In the worst of them, I don't jump off in time.

"I know that," he turns serious. "I was just making a bad joke."

I feel bad for being short with him. Preston has been nothing but nice to me since we broke up. I'm the one with the chip on my shoulder.

"I know you're teasing. Sorry."

He smiles brightly, "No worries." A moment of awkward silence falls over my driveway. "Right, then. I'll let you get to it," he says backing away.

"Hey, Preston?"

He stops and looks hopeful. "Yeah?"

"Thanks for being a good neighbor. It's nice we can still be friendly after everything."

He beams and looks me straight in the eye. "It is nice," he says. "I've missed your wild ways of doing things."

"I don't think I'm that wild," I say.

He cocks his head, "Serial killers, a cult, a kidnapping, not to mention that killer you caught recently. I'd call all that wild."

I notice he only mentioned my victories, not my faults,

or the fact that some people in this town still think of me as a freak.

"I guess I don't live what one would call a regular life," I concede.

"You do what you have to. That's pretty cool. I'm sorry I didn't realize it earlier."

This is as close as we've ever come to discussing our breakup. It's a little much after the run-ins with Lucas today.

I need to run. "Thanks." I don't know what else to say, so I walk to my car and pull the door open.

Preston takes the hint and returns to his side of the driveway. "Okay, then. Have a good run." He waves goodbye.

I start the car and pull down the driveway, not looking at him. I feel his eyes on me as I leave. I try not to think about what our conversation might mean and the fact that he's staring at me through the windshield.

I feel relieved when I drive out of view.

By the time I reach the park, I've pushed the conversation with Preston out of my mind. I want to lose myself in a good hard run. I turn my phone to do not disturb then pull up a playlist I made long ago to run to.

After a quick stretch, I'm headed down the path that winds along the river, my favorite route to go. I jam out to "Nicotine" by Panic at the Disco and run from my problems.

Since I haven't run in months, I'm soon panting and have a stitch in my side. My face is wet with sweat and I have to slow down. I make the turn that takes me by the burned bridge. Workers are repairing the charred remains.

The memory of the explosion bursts in my mind.

I turn away from the bridge, when I see him.

I slow to a stop and stare.

What is he doing here?

Chapter 8

LUCAS

Our work at the scene is done, so we are able to leave a short time later. I'm anxious to get to Gabby with the bracelet. I tell myself it's only because I want information on the case.

I almost believe that.

"Can you drop me at my car?" I ask Dustin once we're back in the cruiser.

He looks at me in surprise. "Where are you going that you need to drive separate? We have a case and a tight deadline."

I pull out the bracelet and show it to Dustin. "It is about the case. This is Shelly Parker's bracelet. I'm hoping Gabby can glean some information from it. Something to help us. We don't have much else, besides a mysterious man in a mask that possibly was at Shelly's last night. I don't know how much I trust the neighbor and what he saw. I also don't know how we're supposed to find the man."

"If it is really a man. If they were dressed head to toe in black, including a hoodie, then it's possible it's a woman."

I think that over. "I suppose it is possible. Although female serial killers are rare."

"But not unheard of. We can't jump to any conclusions at this point."

"All the more reason I need Gabby." I quickly realize I'd said *I* needed her, not *we* needed her. "I mean she can help us." I try to cover my mistake.

Dustin grins knowingly. "Why don't you just apologize and get it over with. You know you want her back."

"I'm not the one that broke us up," I grumble.

"Details. Women don't care about details, they just want a grand gesture."

"I'm not really a grand gesture kind of guy. Besides what if I did that and she still says God wants us apart? How can I argue with that?"

Dustin grows quiet, knowing I'm right.

A few minutes later, he drops me at my car at the station. It's not until I'm pulling out of the parking lot that I realize I don't know where she is, don't know if I should turn left or turn right.

I also don't want to call her.

I send a quick text. "I need your help on the Parker case. Where can I find you?"

I turn left and drive past her shop while I wait for her response. Her car is not in the alley or parked out front, so I keep driving.

She still hasn't responded to my text, so I go to her house. She's most likely there or at Grandma Dot's but her house is closest.

The gray Charger is not in her driveway. I pull in to

60

turn around when I see Preston out on his front steps.

He waves at me, and I'm caught. He'll probably tell Gabby I was here and I'll look like I'm desperate.

I climb out of my car as casually as possible. "Hey," I say. I'm conscious that this looks strange. Me in full uniform, but not in a cruiser, showing up unannounced at her house.

If Preston thinks it's strange that I'm here, he hides it well.

"Detective Hartley, good to see you. What brings you out? Gabby's not here."

"I realize that," I say going for nonchalance. "I need her help on a case. Have you seen her or know where I might find her?"

"Why don't you call her?"

A fair question. "I texted her, but she hasn't answered."

"She probably put her phone on do not disturb. She's out running at the park. She usually turns her phone off and loses herself in music while she runs."

I don't like that Preston knows more about Gabby than I do. At least on this point. To be fair, she hasn't been running much since we've been together.

"At the park, you think?"

"She wanted to see the repairs on the bridge."

I try not to bristle that he knows so much. Are he and Gabby back together? Is that why she broke up with me?

I push that thought away. No matter what's going on, I know Gabby loves me and not her neighbor.

"Thanks," I say and turn on my heel. I feel like an idiot as I hurry back to my car. If she's at the park, I can find her and talk alone.

Workers are repairing the burned bridge when I park in that part of the park. I don't see Gabby's car, but she may have started her run from the other parking lot. I expect she's taking the river path. Lots of runners do.

I start towards the path, and then I see her. She's hard to miss in the bright purple leggings and tank top. She's sweating and winded. Her hair is escaping her ponytail and sticking to her forehead.

She looks beautiful.

Her eyes widen when she sees me. She slows to a stop, then walks slowly my way. The park is nearly empty despite the late afternoon sun. I wish we were completely alone. I wish we were here together. I wish she'd open her mouth and tell me it's all a mistake and she can't live without me.

She opens her mouth, but asks, "Why are you here. Is Dustin okay?"

The question catches me off guard. "Of course he's okay. That's not why I'm here. I texted you earlier. I need your help."

She pulls out her phone and sees my text, then slides the phone back into the pocket on her shapely hip.

"Looks like you found me. How *did* you find me?"

"I stopped by your house and Preston told me where you were."

Did she just blush or is she pink from running?

"Oh. You mentioned the Parker case?" she prompts.

I take out the bracelet and show it to her. "Shelly Parker was wearing this when she was killed. I hoped you could get some information from it."

"So you agree with me now that these are not suicides?" She cocks her head and a curl slides over her forehead. I want to brush it away. Instead, I look at the river.

"I already had a similar thought. Gomez has given us two days to prove it or else she'll rule suicide as manner of death."

"Two days isn't very long."

"I know. That's why I hoped you could help."

She crosses her arms over her chest. "I tried to help earlier and you and that new officer kicked me off the property."

I look at the river again instead of meeting her gaze. "I know. But I'm here now. Will you help?"

She looks at the bracelet and then around the park. "Let's go under that tree over there. I don't want to do this out here in the open."

"Would you like to sit down?" I ask once we are under the tree. "I know this takes a lot out of you."

She flashes her blue eyes at me, then sits without a word. She leans against the tree, takes a deep breath, and pulls off her left glove.

"Let's do this," she says. She closes her eyes and says "Lord, let me see what I need to see." She then takes the bracelet from my hand.

I've seen her do readings many times, but it still freaks me out a bit. She goes stiff and makes a moaning sound. Her face looks terrified, her eyes squeezed tight. She tosses her head from side to side, fast at first, then slowly.

She finally stops moving and slumps against the tree.

She doesn't move for a moment, her eyes still closed. "Gabby? Are you okay?" I've never seen her not come out of it right away.

I shake her bent knee and her eyes flutter open. She looks at me in confusion, then flinches away. "Where are we?"

"We're at the park under a tree."

She sees the bracelet in her hand and throws the chain into the grass. She takes a deep breath and blows it out slowly. "Phew, that was intense," she says trying for a smile but failing.

She's shaking from head to toe, her face pale. "What happened? You usually come out of a vision without a problem. I couldn't wake you up."

"That's because she couldn't wake up. He forced her to take them," she jerks as a shiver runs through her. "He shoved the pills in her mouth and forced her to swallow them. It was awful."

She sits forward suddenly and I think she's going to throw up, but she just coughs and gags. "I can't get the taste of the pills out of my mouth, or the smell of the hand on my face."

I feel terrible for putting her through this. "I'm sorry, Gabby. I didn't know it would be so horrible for you."

She lifts her head and looks me in the eye. "It is. I always is. I see them die, Lucas. I live through their murder. It's not fun."

I can't hold her gaze. I'd never thought of it like that. I'd just thought of how cool it was that she can do it. "I'm

64

sorry," I say, knowing it's not enough.

She climbs to her feet and brushes grass from her rear. "Don't worry about it. No one else gets it, either."

I retrieve the bracelet from the grass and run it through my fingers. I close my eyes a moment and listen to the wind, wondering if I can get a reading from the bracelet, if there's some kind of magic in it.

No magic. It's just a chain of metal, nothing more. The magic is Gabby.

"Did you see the man or woman that did it?" I ask hopefully.

She pulls her ponytail tie from her hair and curls cascade around her face. "No. I didn't see his face exactly. He's wearing a mask of some sort. A white, blank face mask. It's very creepy."

"You sure it's a man?"

She scrunches her face in thought. "I'm not sure, now that you mention it. He, or she, doesn't say anything. They are strong. Shelly fought hard, but she couldn't get the hands off her face."

"A strong person that may or may not be a man," I muse. "And a mask. That matches what the witness saw."

"You have a witness?"

"A neighbor saw someone leaving her house late last night. Dressed in loose black clothes and wearing a white mask like you saw."

"So you already knew that she was murdered and someone saw the killer?"

I nod.

"Yet, you track me down to do a reading and see the

65

same thing?"

"I guess."

"Knowing how hard these readings are on me? Knowing I would see something horrible?"

"I didn't think of it like that. I just want to solve this case and I knew you could help."

She looks around. "If this was actually about the case, Dustin would be with you."

I don't have an answer for that. Why didn't I come with Dustin?

The wind blows a curl into her lips and she tucks it behind her ear. "You sure you didn't just want to see me?"

I look up into the tree in exasperation. "Fine, I wanted to see you," I snap. "You broke it off last week with no warning. You handed me the necklace I gave you and sent me away. No explanation other than your tattoo told you to."

She lifts her chin stubbornly. "God told me to do it."

"But why? We haven't even discussed any of this. You just disappeared."

"I don't know why. I just have to trust that He has his reasons. And I didn't disappear. I've been right here the whole time. Where have you been?"

"Where have I been?" My voice is rising and I can't stop it. "*You* broke it off, *you* have to fix it."

"You really want me to fix it or do you want that new officer, Kalissta Hawthorne?"

I nearly fall over in shock. Gabby's jealous?

"There is nothing between me and Officer Hawthorne. That's ridiculous."

66

"Don't call me ridiculous. I saw her with you this morning. I don't have to be psychic to know she wants you. And you put your hand on her arm and then basically told me to get lost. What am I supposed to think?"

She is panting in anger, her chest rising and falling under her distractingly tiny tank top.

"What about you and Preston? He seemed to know a lot about you today. Is that what this is all about? You want to get back with him?"

Her head snaps like she's been hit. "Preston? You're going to bring him into this?" she hisses. "Preston is just my neighbor."

"He'd like to be more. I can tell."

"Well, that's his problem," she snaps.

We stand in silence, both of us breathing hard. I want to take her into my arms and kiss some sense into her.

Our eyes lock and for a moment, a lovely moment, I see she still loves me. It burns in her eyes, replaces the anger. Her shoulders relax and she takes a tiny step in my direction.

She freezes and claps her hand over her tattoo.

Then takes a step back.

"Seriously?" I ask in disbelief. "Again with the *'message from God'*?"

Now her eyes are full of fury. "If you don't believe me, maybe it's best if you go and don't come back." She sounds so sad, so disappointed.

Do I believe? Is that the issue?

I don't know how to answer. I open my mouth, but no words come out.

She hangs her head. "Okay, then, I'll go. If you need any more help with the case, send Dustin."

She jogs away, sticking her earbuds back in her ears. I watch her as she breaks into a sprint. She pounds the path that leads back to the other parking lot. As I watch, she turns the corner and disappears.

I should chase after her. I know I should. Instead, I look to the sky. "Why?" I ask the clouds.

In answer, I suddenly want my sister, Crystal. I think of her often, but I haven't been to her grave since her memorial.

I need to see her grave.

Is this how God works, random thoughts that cannot be ignored?

I ponder that question as I drive away from the park.

Chapter 9

GABBY

I pound the path hard with my sneakers on the way back to my car. I can't believe Lucas would use me and my abilities like that. Unbidden, tears threaten my eyes. I wipe angrily at my face.

I will not cry over him again.

Maybe God is right. If he can't trust me, believe in what I see or hear, then I'm better off without him.

"Better off without him," I mutter, trying to believe it myself by repeating the phrase.

My tattoo again told me, not yet.

Yet. That means we have a future.

What kind of future can I have with him second guessing me?

I'm winded and sweating hard when I reach my car. I open the door and dig out a bottle of water from the back floorboard where random bottles and cans roll around. The water is warm, but I down it in one long series of gulps.

I wipe water from my lips and take deep breaths until the stitch in my side subsides. The sun is dipping toward the horizon and my soul is tired. I want to go home.

I try not to think of Lucas as I drive home. Try not to

think of the murder I saw in the bracelet. Try not to think at all.

The not thinking works fairly well for a while, until I turn on the news later. Lacey fills the screen as she talks about the suicides and accidents that seem suspicious. The video accompanying her story is of me talking with Lucas, Dustin, and that new officer, Kalissta Hawthorne. The camera zooms close as I lose my temper and jump at Hawthorne. The shameful moment of lost control plays over the air for all the town to see. My cheeks burn alone on my couch. Now that I see it, I overreacted.

The house suddenly feels stifling and I long for the night air. On my back porch, I have a small fire pit. In my current low mood, a fire seems just the ticket.

A small while later, I'm settled in a chair near the small fire, a can of Dr. Pepper in one hand, the other stroking Chester on my lap. I lean back in the chair and look to the stars. As always, the stars make me feel small, and make my worries seem insignificant.

Losing Lucas doesn't feel insignificant. A murderer on the loose doesn't feel insignificant.

But the stars are vast. The moon has seen heartbreak and murder before. I relax as I let the weight of my concerns float away. My eyes drift closed and I listen to the night bugs and frogs sing, to the crackle of the fire. For a moment, I'm one with the universe.

Footsteps on gravel interrupt the moment.

The steps grow closer and my eyes fly open.

They are coming down the alley towards my back patio. The sound stops at Preston's back yard. A shadow looms near a tree there.

I sit up straight, Chester hisses at the shape.

"Gabby?"

It's Preston. He steps from the shadow of his tree. He's wearing a black hoodie and dark jeans and blends into the darkness.

"Preston? What are you doing out here so late?"

He walks to the chain link fence between our back yards. "I was just out for a walk."

He doesn't seem nervous, although I find it suspicious that he'd walk in the dark, especially down the alley behind our houses.

"Want some company?" he asks hopefully.

I can't think of a reason to tell him no without sounding rude, so I invite him over.

He takes the empty seat next to me. The seat Lucas once sat in a few weeks ago when we had a fire here together.

It feels strange to have Preston so close, so chummy.

"Phew, I worked up a sweat," he says and pulls the hoodie off. Up close, I can see it is dark blue, not black. He wears a white t-shirt underneath. He leans back in his chair, makes himself comfortable. "Did you have a good run?" he asks.

I lean back, too, and settle into my seat, my eyes fixed on the fire. "I did. It was good to work out some of the tension from the last few days." I expect him to mention telling Lucas where I was, but he changes the subject.

"I saw you on the news."

"Yeah. Not my best moment."

71

"At least Lacey Aniston didn't make fun of you."

"We're on good terms now," I say then take a swig of my Dr. Pepper. "She promised not to do that anymore."

Preston looks longingly at my drink. "You want one?"

"Do you have any beer?"

"Just sodas."

"Then I'll be right back." He disappears into his yard. Chester has relaxed on my lap and I stroke him behind the ears as I wait.

I don't wait long and Preston returns with two bottles of beer.

"Maybe something stronger than soda will make you feel better."

I take the bottle and twist the cap off, then take a sip. The cold beer feels good on my tongue.

Preston takes a long drink from his bottle, then clinks it against mine. "Here's to a lovely night and a nice fire."

I toast to that and take another drink.

It feels good to relax, to just be. He tells me about an eccentric client he had at the car dealership and I tell him about a reading I did on an old watch the other day. Before I know it, we've had more than one beer and the moon has slid across the sky.

The streets are quiet, only a few cars out this late. I throw another log on the fire and sit back.

I feel Preston's eyes on me as the firelight flickers across my face. I'm slightly giddy from the beer and relaxed for a change.

"You really are beautiful," he says suddenly.

I meet his eyes in shock and don't know what to say.

I'm no longer relaxed.

The fire crackles for a few long moments, then I stammer, "Look, Preston."

"I know. I know. I blew it and it's too late for us. I just wanted you to know I'm sorry for how it ended."

"But it did end. We're just friends now."

He looks away and into the fire.

"Friends is better than nothing," he says and downs the rest of his beer.

I have no idea what to do or how to save the evening. What was so comfortable and soothing just moments before is now awkward.

Sipping my beer, I don't say anything.

After a few moments of silence, he stands and stretches. "Thanks for the nice evening," he says, gathering the empty bottles up. "I'll just throw these in my recycling."

I stand too, my head a bit fuzzy.

He looks at me seriously and for a moment, I'm afraid he might try to kiss me.

I don't want him to and he must sense it.

"Okay, then. Good night, Gabby."

He tosses his dark hoodie over his shoulder and is gone around to the front of our houses. I wait until I hear his door close, then I look at Chester.

"That was awkward," I say to the cat.

He licks a paw and ignores me.

Chapter 10

LUCAS

I flip Shelly Parker's bracelet through my fingers as I drive to the cemetery where my sister, Crystal, is buried. I have not visited her new grave in the months since her memorial service.

I'm not sure why I need to see her now.

She isn't really here, but I need to talk to her.

The cemetery is small and quiet, situated on the edge of town, a tiny church nearby. I never understood why Dad had her re-buried here. He said that he attended the little church as a child. As I stare at the church, I can't imagine going to services here. When I do get the chance to go to church, I like the larger church out on Highway 7. This little church feels like it is lost in time, with a couple dozen graves surrounding it.

The newest of them is Crystal's.

Dad had a tasteful headstone put up and I find it easily.

Her name is cut into the stone and the dates of her birth and her murder.

Tears burn the back of my throat as I kneel by the stone.

Now that I'm here, I'm not sure what to do. I came to terms with losing my sister years ago when she disappeared.

"Hey, Sis," I say out loud, feeling foolish. "This is a nice place for you to rest in." I swallow against the emotions that bubble up.

How do I talk to her?

Why do I need to?

"So sorry for what happened to you," I try again.

The grave is silent and so are my tears.

"This is dumb," I say, standing. "You're not actually here. You've been gone for years."

I don't want to feel like this. I want to get back to work on the Parker case. I want to have Gabby back. I want life to go back to normal.

Whatever normal is.

"She left me," I say quietly. "Or closer to the truth, I chased her away. I didn't understand what she was hearing, what she goes through."

The engraved headstone glitters slightly in the dipping sun, but doesn't make me feel better.

Maybe I don't deserve to feel better.

"Well, I don't know what else to say." I wipe my eyes in frustration.

Why am I here?

A car crunches gravel as it pulls into the lot and parks next to my car. I feel very conspicuous here in my uniform talking to a piece of granite.

A man makes his way up the walk to the tiny church. He eyes me with friendly curiosity and gives me a little wave.

I wave back, then have an urge to talk to the man.

I say goodbye to Crystal, then head to the church. Stone steps lead to the double doors of the church. I hesitate outside and peek into the windows. From here, I can see the entire inside of the church. The man is walking between the pews, straightening hymnals.

I hear words in my head, "Talk to him."

I look around as if I'll see someone behind me. I know I won't.

The words are from God.

I pull the handle on the door and the quiet of the church descends on me as I walk inside.

The man looks up as if he expected to see me.

"Hello," he says in an inviting way. "I'm Pastor Jackson."

I slowly walk down the center aisle. "Hello, I hope I'm not intruding."

"Not at all," the man comes from between the pews and motions for me to take a seat in the front row. "How can I help you?"

"How do you know I need help?"

He cocks his head, "Most people that come in here on a random evening are looking for something. What are you looking for?" he asks enigmatically.

Sitting in the front pew, I look up at the large cross hanging above the altar. "I guess I'm looking for guidance."

The man sits across the aisle from me and looks at the cross too. "Guidance in what way?"

"How do you know when God is talking to you?" I didn't know that was the question I was going to ask.

"Hmm, that's a tough one. It's different for each of us." I'm happy he keeps his eyes on the front of the room. I feel sort of silly talking like this.

But I press on. "What does it sound like?"

"For me, it's like an impulse to do something or say something. An impulse I don't quite understand, but I can't deny."

"Like when I had the urge to come here?"

"Could be. Here you are."

"My girlfriend get's clear messages from God."

"That's wonderful that she's learned to listen."

I make a sarcastic sound. "Oh, she listens. She listens and obeys. That's why she broke up with me."

"It's a rare gift to hear messages so clearly. She is very lucky. Why do you think God told her to break it off with you?"

I think on this, staring at the fading sun shining on the cross. "I didn't believe the way I should."

"Do you believe now?"

Do I?

"I'm here. I obeyed."

"Obedience is only part of the equation. You have to believe in what you are obeying. Maybe that is what God is trying to teach you. If your girlfriend truly gets messages, it will take a man with a strong faith to be with her. What she must obey affects you as well. Can you be that man?"

I inhale sharply, knowing he's spoken a truth.

"I want to be that man. I want to do that for God and for her." I swallow hard, emotion swamping me. "And for me."

Pastor Jackson moves across the aisle to sit next to me. He pats me on the shoulder. "If you truly want that, all you have to do is ask God."

My throat burns as I ask, "Is it that simple?"

He laughs softly, "Nothing about giving your life to God is simple."

I make another sarcastic sound. "Yeah. Gabby's life has not been simple since she started listening and doing what the messages say." I feel a tear slide down my cheek. I feel full. I feel fulfilled. I feel ready.

I stand on shaking legs, my belt jangling loudly in the hush of the church. It's only two steps to the altar rail. The most important steps of my life.

I drop to my knees and bow my head, my hands clasped on the rail.

Pastor Jackson kneels next to me, his hand on my back.

Sobs shake out of me as the Spirit floods my soul. "God, I give myself to you, fully and completely," I whisper. "Thank you for showing me the true way."

The pastor takes over the praying and blesses me on my journey with Christ. The magnitude of what I just did fills me with peace, with joy. When he says Amen, I raise my wet eyes to him.

"I have to tell Gabby that I understand now." I can't wait to see her. Can't wait to tell her.

"Go to her."

I climb from my knees and fairly float out of the church. On my way to my car, I stop by Crystal's grave again.

"I did it, Sis. I gave myself to God."

The sunset burns red and orange, a celebration of color that matches the celebration in my heart.

The headstone glitters again and I feel like Crystal is proud of me, is looking down from heaven and blessing me.

I turn my face to the sunset and whisper, "Thank you."

I want to drive straight to Gabby, but I have three texts from Dustin and one voicemail. "Chief Simmons is looking for you," is the gist of the texts. He sounds annoyed in the voicemail.

"Where are you? We have a case and only two days to solve it."

My high from the church fades. As much as I want to run to Gabby, the case must come first.

Dustin is at his desk when I return to the station. He looks up, his face pinched. "Where have you been? Simmons is breathing down my neck. He agrees with us after I told him about the witness."

"I had some personal things to take care of."

He searches my face. "Something's different. You look lighter, but your eyes are red."

I wipe at them, self-consciously. "Yeah, I am different. Do you remember when you gave yourself to God?"

Dustin looks surprised at my question. We don't normally talk like this. "Is this about Gabby?"

I notice he didn't answer my question. "In a way. I was just at that church out on Brown Road and I had the most wonderful moment at the altar."

I'm not sure if I expect him to laugh or not. I just feel so full of the spirit, I need to share.

"I did that at the church camp Grandma Dot made us go to. I didn't enjoy the camp, didn't get it. Then one night, it was different. That explains the red eyes. I cried like a baby."

I stare at my best friend, feeling closer to him than I ever have.

"Yeah," I say wistfully. "Pretty amazing."

Simmons enters the office then, and the mood changes. "Hartley, where have you been? I've been looking for you."

"Sorry, Chief. I was taking care of something. I'm here now."

"Well, okay then," he says hesitantly.

"What's up?" I ask.

"Hawthorne finished her canvas of Shelly Parker's neighborhood. As usual, no one wanted to talk. She did manage to get a statement about a white car that was parked down the street for the last few days. The woman who reported it says she's sure it didn't belong to anyone in the neighborhood. Was there at different times of the day and night, but no one got out of it."

"So someone was casing her house," I say.

"Looks like it."

"A white car isn't very descriptive. Did the witness say anything else?" Dustin asks.

"Just that it was a four door. I know it's not much, but it's all we have so far. Did you get anything back on the pill bottle?"

Dustin shakes his head, "Not yet. The label was torn off. It's not that hard to get pills on that street, though."

"Well, keep working. If there really is a serial killer in town, we can't rest until we catch them."

I'm torn between the need to work and the need to see Gabby.

Work has to win for now.

But the late night has to end at some point.

Then I'm driving straight to her house and I'm not leaving until we are back together.

I smile at the thought. She's going to be so excited when she realizes I trust in God the same as her. That has to win her back.

It's been a few frustrating hours at the station. Dustin and I worked hard, but we didn't make any progress on the case. We really have little to go on. We managed to look into Shelly Parker's past, but little else.

Finally, we called it quits for the night.

Finally, I'm headed to see Gabby.

Excitement swirls in my belly at the prospect of seeing her again. In my head, I practice what I'm going to say. I have to get the words right.

Her neighborhood is dark at this late hour, except for a few porch lights. I park in front of her house and quietly shut the door.

Her porch light is not on and I don't see light inside. I do see flickering coming from between her and Preston's house.

Fire.

Worried, I hurry between the garages to the back yard.

I stop when I see the small porch fire pit, when I see her sitting with Preston, all cozy.

"You really are beautiful," he says.

I feel like I've been punched in the gut.

Before I hear anything else, I sneak away. I dart for my car and drive.

My heart aches. My stomach hurts.

"You really are beautiful." Those are words I should be saying, not him.

All kinds of responses play out in my mind. The worst one ending with Gabby taking him into her house.

My mouth goes dry at the thought.

A knife seems to twist in my side.

"Too late," I whisper. "I'm too late."

Chapter 11

According to the news, the inept River Bend Police Department has finally made the connection. They finally realize I've been at work in their midst.

Judging by the video accompanying the story, She finally has caught on, too. She is why I do this. She is the true target.

Cleaning up the town is a bonus. I want Her.

The thought of it makes my blood burn. I need to finish this. I need to continue.

I search through my collection until I find what I need. The blade that I've been waiting to use. The final test for Her.

The pills were fun. I enjoyed the struggle to get them down her throat.

The untraceable guns are less fun. The moment is over too quickly. A pull of the trigger and they are gone. But guns are the easiest to fake the scene with, so I use them.

But the blade is the best. I enjoy the blade. As I hold it in my hand, a rush or excitement flows through me. I need to use it.

I had intended to wait. But the game is afoot now. She

knows I'm here. She hunts for me.

Tonight, I will hunt.

I have one job left. One more poor soul that is dirtying up this town. One that should have stayed home.

And it will draw Her out.

Chapter 12

KALISSTA HAWTHORNE

I find myself on the couch and don't remember how I got here.

It happened again.

I scrub at my eyes and blink several times. The room comes into focus.

How did I get on the couch?

Since I've come to River Bend, the spells like this have gotten worse.

When my Great Aunt Pauline set me up with a job on the police force, I thought this would be a good place to start over.

But the spells returned, instead of getting better.

My t-shirt is soaked in sweat and my blood is pounding.

Was that the rattle of my front door?

I jump off the couch and run to the front window. I sneak a peek through a gap in the curtain, but all I see is my own reflection.

My hair is a mess.

Did I take my bun out?

I don't remember doing it, but my hair is loose and mussed up now. I run my fingers through it and find a small twig caught in the strands.

When did I go outside?

I take a steadying breath. "You're okay. You're okay," I repeat the mantra the counselor taught me.

Wait, that isn't it.

"I'm okay. I'm okay."

Yes that's it. "Take ownership of your feelings," she'd said. "Only then can you control them."

Silly woman. Control is a myth.

I learned that before the Army. I'd hoped the structure of the military would offer me some peace.

I was wrong.

Dead wrong.

Don't think of that now.

The rattle of the door again. I turn around quickly, flip on the front light and look out the flimsy curtain. This time, I pull the curtain back in a swift swoop, sure I'll see whoever is trying to get to me.

The front steps are empty.

"I'm okay," I start again.

I don't feel okay.

Sure there is no one in the front yard, I go to my bathroom and find the pills that I hate to take. The pills make me tired, slow my reflexes.

They also soothe my mind.

I open the bottle and down two of them dry.

Staring into the mirror, I repeat the mantra. I focus on the browns of my eyes, the pupils are huge.

"Just get control," I change the mantra to one I feel better with. Control. I need control.

After I wash my face and run a brush through my hair, I feel a bit better. The pills are kicking in.

If I take a third one, I'll really feel better.

"No more than two at a time," the psychiatrist said. "You can't medicate PTSD away."

PTSD.

I hate the letters.

How can you boil the mess inside me down to four letters?

I flip off the switch and stand in the darkness. When I close the door, I'm surrounded by pitch blackness.

Only now can I take a deep breath.

In the darkness, I can relax.

He floats into my mind like he does several times a day. His blue eyes, and the way they crinkle when he smiles dances through my head.

Such a pretty color. Such handsome eyes.

His broad shoulders as he walks across the bull pen at work when he doesn't know I'm watching.

His voice as it carries out of his office into the hall where I find myself too many times a day.

I think of him and my heart calms.

The door on the bathroom shakes.

I scream and throw the door open.

My hall is empty.

I press my hands to my head, willing the hallucinations to stop.

I need him.

I rush into the bedroom, looking for my phone. I can't find it. I flip the tightly made blankets off the bed, looking for it. Nothing.

I search the drawer of my nightstand and don't find it.

The front door rattles.

"Go away!" I scream.

I need him. I need to see him. He can fix me.

Giving up my search of the bedroom, I go to the kitchen and find my phone in the center of my dining table.

I have no memory of how it got there.

The last time I used it was to return Aunt Pauline's message reminding me of her party. That was in the bedroom.

How did the phone get here?

Deciding I don't care, I grab it and dial the number I entered into the memory a few weeks ago. As I press the call button, I hope he doesn't wonder how I got his number. He didn't give it to me. I found it in the directory at the station.

"Hartley," he answers on the fourth ring. He sounds tired. My heart goes out to him. I could make him feel better if he'd just let me. I'd take better care of him than that freak ever did.

"Detective Hartley, this is Kalissta Hawthorne," I start.

"Hawthorne? What's the matter?" I wish he'd used my first name, but we will get to that.

"I think someone is trying to break into my house."

"Why didn't you call dispatch?"

A fair question. "I didn't want it to get around the station. But I'm a little freaked out right now." I keep talking so he can't stop me and hang up. "Would you mind, terribly, coming over and checking things out? I know I shouldn't be scared, but I am."

I turn on all the charm I can muster, hoping he'll fall for the damsel in distress gambit. Knowing him like I do, I'm fairly sure he will.

He sighs heavily, but agrees to come over.

I won the first round.

Take that, Gabby.

Chapter 13

LUCAS

The last thing I want to do tonight is go help Hawthorne. I want to stay home and lick my wounds over Gabby. After the high of the church, the low of finding her with Preston hits like a sucker punch.

I hate that I ran away like a scared boy. I should have confronted them. I should have stood up for her.

Instead, I came home, opened a beer, and went to bed, her necklace clutched in my hand.

Stupid. I'm stupid.

I drag myself from bed and pull on jeans and a t-shirt. Gabby's necklace is still in my hand and I slide it into my pocket along with my phone. I tuck my service pistol and badge into the pockets of my jacket.

I throw the half-empty beer bottle in the trash and tell myself I can have another when I get back from helping Hawthorne.

It shouldn't take long. She lives only a few blocks away. I'll do a quick check of her house and come back home to feel sorry for myself.

The front porch light is on at her house. In fact, all the

lights are on. The rest of the block is dark at this hour, and her house fairly glows in the cloudy night. I park on the street and walk up the short driveway past her white car. I search the shadows for any sign of an intruder or a peeping tom or anyone suspicious.

The yard is clear, so I make my way to the back, my gun held at the ready, just in case.

The backyard is much darker than the front. No porch light here and clouds block the moon. I don't find anything out of the ordinary and make my way back to the front of the house.

Hawthorne is waiting for me on the porch.

I tuck my gun back into my jacket pocket.

"I'm so glad you came," she says breathlessly. "I know I should have checked it out myself, but I was so scared." She tilts her head and makes her eyes wide. "Did you see anything?"

"All clear," I say from the bottom of the porch steps. "You sure someone was here?"

"I thought I heard someone rattling the door knob. It was locked, of course." I notice she's looking past me, not at me.

"Well, if they were here, they are gone now."

"You're the best, Lucas," she coos. "Come in and I'll get you a drink."

She steps into the house before I can refuse her. I'm left alone at the bottom of the steps. If I leave now, I'll look rude.

I take the three steps up, creaking on the second one, and cross the porch. I step through the open door and enter a house like I've never seen.

Military memorabilia crowds every wall. Guns and knives hang on display as well as pictures and maps.

"Wow," I say before I can stop myself.

She watches me from the kitchen. "Like my collection?"

"Yeah. Where did you get all this stuff?"

"I've collected it since I was a girl. I spent four years in the Army and it just made my interest stronger. Beer or soda? I have both."

"Soda," I say absently, looking closer at a map of the South Pacific. "This is really impressive."

She hands me a can of Pepsi, "I guess. I'm kind of used to it." She tries to sound casual about it, but the pride in her voice is obvious.

I cross the room to a display case full of knives hanging on small nails. She follows close behind, her body almost touching mine as I lean over the case. "There's one missing," I say, touching the glass of the case.

Hawthorne goes stiff beside me. "So there is." She leans closer to the glass as if she can't believe one is gone. "That's odd." She looks around the room. "I must have moved it." Her face is flushed and her hand shakes a little as she sips her Pepsi.

I move on to another case, this one full of antique pistols. "Wow," I say again. We spend the next half hour talking about the collection. I feel the tension slip from my shoulders as I talk guns and ammo with her. She's quite knowledgeable and I learn a lot.

I finally realize how late it is. I pull my phone from my pocket to check the time and it brings Gabby's necklace out with it. I tuck the chain and entwined hearts back in my pocket quickly, but she notices.

"That's quite a necklace there," she says softly. "Is it Gabby's?"

"Yes, it was."

"Hmm."

"What's that supposed to mean?"

"Just everyone thinks you got the raw end of the deal with that one. You have always been such a supporter of hers, to the detriment of your own reputation and career. Then she drops you. It's not fair."

"Everyone says?"

"Those that care." She dips her head and looks up through her lashes as she steps closer. She couldn't be more obvious.

I try to step back, but bump into a glass case full of grenades from years past. The case shakes when I hit it.

"Lucas, I'm not going to hurt you," she smiles at my discomfort.

"It's Detective Hartley."

"You can call me Kalissta. In fact, I wish you would." Her voice holds an invitation.

"Officer Hawthorne, I'm sorry, but-,"

"Shhh," she suddenly leans forward and places her lips on mine. The display case blocks my escape.

I'm so shocked, it takes a moment for me to react. She takes that moment as interest and deepens the kiss.

I grab her by both wrists and push her away. She

stumbles backward and pulls her hands from my grip.

A grin creeps onto her face and she wipes at her mouth. "It's going to be like that is it?"

"I'm sorry," I try for politeness.

"Always the gentleman." Her voice is heavy with disdain. "Gabby is a fool in addition to a freak."

I drop all politeness at that. "Do not talk about Gabby. She is twice the woman you could ever be."

"You barely know me."

"I know you faked an intruder to lure me over here tonight."

She laughs suddenly. "Way to go, Detective. You solved the case."

I push past her out of the room. She follows me to the front door.

"I'm sorry," she simpers suddenly. "I shouldn't have said that. Don't go." She leans against the door to block my exit.

"Move."

"Not while you're mad at me. I'm sorry. I've had a really bad night. See, I'm not well."

"I don't want to hear it." I reach behind her for the door handle. I'll make her move if I have to.

"Don't leave like this. I'm sorry, Lucas."

I can't believe this begging woman is the same one that tried to kiss me only moments ago. Maybe she really isn't well.

"I'm not mad," I say gently. "I just think it's better if I go."

"Stay. We can keep talking about my collection. I have

a whole other room I haven't shown you."

As impressed with the collection as I was, I'm starting to find it a little disturbing to be alone with her with so many weapons nearby.

"Officer Hawthorne, let me out."

"Kalissta. My name is Kalissta."

I give in. Whatever it takes to escape. "Kalissta, please let me out. I'm not mad. I promise. I'm just tired and need to go home." I use my softest voice. The one I use on my daughter Olivia when she's upset.

She steps away from the door.

"Promise, you're not mad?"

"I promise."

She opens the door and I hurry onto the porch. "And I'll see you at work?"

"Yes, you will," I continue with the soft voice that seems to be working.

She suddenly grins that creepy grin again. "Not if I see you first." She then slams the door.

I don't stop to think about what that might mean. I walk quickly to my car and climb in. The porch light goes out before I can start the car. Then her house goes dark while I'm pulling away.

I'm not comfortable with her alone with the guns and the knives now that I know she's unstable.

And she wears a gun at work.

How did she ever get on the force to begin with? Should I tell Chief Simmons about my concerns?

Tell him what? That she tried to kiss me? I can't see me saying those words out loud. That will be a secret I keep.

A shameful secret.

I speed the few blocks home and let myself into my house. Opening the fridge, I take out a beer and drain half of it in one go. The cool liquid swims in my belly, washes away the taste of Hawthorne's lips on mine.

I pull Gabby's necklace from my pocket and run it through my fingers as I return to my bedroom and my bed.

I'm beat. Just beat.

It has been an emotionally draining day.

I hang the chain and entwined hearts on the lamp near my bed and lie down. I stare at the glimmering necklace for a few minutes.

I think of the wonder of giving myself to God earlier. *Everything will soon be righted.*

I relax into the bed at the thought.

As I turn out the light, I hear rain on the roof. Lightening brightens my room, followed several seconds later by the roll of thunder.

"Storm's not too close, yet," I say to the necklace as I fall asleep.

Chapter 14

GABBY

I dream of Lucas. We are walking in the field behind Grandma Dot's house, his hand in mine. The necklace he gave me for Christmas is heavy on my neck, a welcome weight. I touch it with my fingertip. He stops and turns to me, love shining in his eyes. His hands are on my hips and he pulls me close. He leans in for a kiss.

Thunder shakes my small house, waking me from the lovely dream. I blink into the dark, my mind taking a moment to realize I'm alone in my bed, not with Lucas in the field.

I groan in disappointment and roll over. Chester scurries away from the bed. I stare at the wall and listen to the rain beating on the roof. Lightening brightens my room, followed by the crash of thunder.

The air is full of electricity.

My tattoo is sizzling.

Go to him.

I don't believe the words. I've waited for a week for a sign that this separation will end, that I can be reunited with the man I love more than anything.

Go to him.

Now? In the middle of a storm?

I don't care. If God says it's time, I'm more than ready.

I toss the covers back and grab jeans and a jacket and pull on some shoes.

Less than a minute from when I got the first message, I'm running through the pelting rain to my Charger.

The rain pounds the car and the wipers squeak loudly as they toss across the windshield. I drive faster than the weather should allow. Lightening bathes the town in light. Thunder shakes the car.

My heart is racing and my mind is a tumult.

What will I say when I get there? How will I explain this middle of the night flight to his door?

I get the feeling he won't want to hear that my tattoo told me to go.

As I pull into his neighborhood, I slow to a crawl.

Seriously, what am I going to say? Hi, I made a mistake. It wasn't a mistake. I don't know why we had to be apart, but I know there is a reason.

As I creep down his block, I realize that the entire street is dark. There isn't a single porch light on. Not one window is lit up. Even the street lights aren't on.

The storm must have knocked the power out.

There are few cars parked on the street, but a white four-door a little way down from his driveway catches my attention. As I watch, a dark, hooded figure climbs out and sneaks through his yard.

As the wipers clear my view the figure disappears into his backyard. I park a few yards away from the white car, pull the hood of my jacket up and climb into the rain.

I slide off my left glove as I approach the car. I wrap

my bare fingers around the wet door handle.

The impressions hit instantly, a repeating phrase.

If I can't have him, no one can. If I can't have him, no one can.

I force myself to release the handle, disturbed by the unstable mania of the vision. I have no doubt who him is.

Lucas is in danger.

I reach for my phone, but I forgot it in my haste to get here.

"Crap on a cracker," I say into the rain and follow the figure into the backyard.

I stay close to the wall, ducking behind bushes as I go. When I reach the corner of the house, I peek around. The mysterious person is pacing the back patio, gesturing wildly.

Lightning brightens the sky and for a moment, I can see her clearly.

It's the new officer, Kalissta Hawthorne.

I can also see the gun in her hand.

I want to jump from my hiding place and tackle her. I have the element of surprise, but I know better than to confront a mad woman with a gun when I'm unarmed. I don't even see any sticks to use.

The pounding rain lets up and I can hear her mumbling to herself.

"I can't do this. I shouldn't do this." Then in a deeper voice. "I need to do this. He can't reject me and get away with it."

I wonder what Lucas and she have been up to that would elicit this response, but I don't have time to worry about it now. She's flailing the gun around recklessly and she's near the window I know leads to his bedroom. Even if she shot into the wall from the outside, he could be hurt.

Water seeps through my jacket hood and drips down my face. I wipe it away with the back of my hand.

The small motion catches her attention and her head whips in my direction.

"Who's there?" she shouts. "Lucas?" The hopeful note in her voice is pitiful.

I duck behind the bush again.

Lightning cracks nearby and I'm exposed for her to see.

"Gabby? What in the world are you doing here?" she shouts. I can barely hear her over the thunder.

I stay behind the bush, and shout as loud as I can, hoping to wake Lucas. "Kalissta, you don't want to do this. Put down the gun."

She laughs wildly, tossing her head back so her hood falls down. Her long hair is soon soaked with rain.

"Put down the gun," I shout again.

"I don't take orders from you. I'm the cop. You're just the freak."

I let the comment pass over me. I've been called worse. "Lucas wouldn't want you to do this," I try.

"Lucas is no longer your concern. What are you even doing here? Did you have a vision?" She makes vision sound like a dirty word.

"What if I did?"

"That just proves you're a freak." She is stepping closer, is only a few feet from the bush between us.

Lightning crashes again and I see the patio door behind her is sliding open. I also see the gun is leveled at me.

"If I can't have him, you can't either," she shouts between the flash and the thunder. When the rumble comes, the patio door flies open and Lucas rushes her from behind.

The gun goes off, the flash bright in the dark.

Chapter 15

GABBY

I brace for the hit, but the bullet zips past my ear.

Kalissta hits the ground with Lucas on top of her. In a moment, he has the gun away from her and her hands twisted behind her back.

He looks up at me. "You okay?" Even in the dark, I can see the concern.

I nod and say, "It missed me. Barely."

"Go get my cuffs and call Dustin."

I rush into the house and to the counter where I know he keeps his cuffs when he's not working. I'm not sure where his phone is, probably by his bed. I jog down the hall to his room and search in the dark on the night stand.

My hand bumps the lamp and I see something glimmer a little. Another flash of lightning and I see my necklace hanging from the lamp. The sight of it makes me smile. He's obviously been missing me.

I touch the necklace and make it swing, my heart full of love.

I then grab the phone and head back outside.

Once Kalissta is cuffed and secure, he sits her up. "What in the world were you thinking?" Lucas demands. "Coming here with a gun."

Kalissta hangs her head, her wet hair blocks her face.

"She said if she couldn't have you, then no one could," I tell him.

Her head snaps up.

"I never said that."

"You thought it. I read it from your door handle on your car."

She twists her face into a look of disgust. "Freak! You are not worthy of him."

I step closer and crouch before her. In a voice I'm impressed I can control, I say, "If you call me a freak one more time, I will slap that face of yours. Do you understand?"

She stares me straight in the eye. And then I see it. Fear.

The fear hurts more than the freak comment.

She shivers and I tell myself it's from the cold rain, not from being so close to me.

Lucas takes the phone from my hand and dials Dustin. He leaves Kalissta sitting on the wet ground as he places the call. She keeps her eyes on him, occasionally darting a look at me. It's blatantly obvious she thinks she's in love with him.

I resist the urge to touch him, to show her he belongs to me. Instead, I step between them so she can only see me.

"We have a problem," Lucas is saying to Dustin. "Officer Hawthorne showed up at my house with a gun."

I can hear Dustin cuss on the other end of the line.

"Gabby is here, too." Lucas pauses. "I don't know

why, exactly. But I think she saved my life."

Kalissta wriggles uncomfortably on the ground, rain running unchecked down her face. "I wasn't really going to shoot you," she says.

I roll my eyes so she can see. "Right. You just snuck around back with a gun to say hi."

She glares at me.

"No one asked you. It's none of your business."

"When you shot at me, it became my business," I hiss.

Lucas steps between us and says, "Dustin's on his way." He looks down at Kalissta. "What were you thinking? This will destroy you."

She cocks her head and looks up through her eyelashes. Even in the dark, I can recognize the flirty look. "Only if you turn me in. You can let me go and we can pretend this never happened."

I make a sound of disgust. "Yeah, right. You fired a gun in a residential neighborhood. Who knows what else you would have done if I didn't come."

"I was here as a guest and thought I saw someone lurking behind a bush. In the dark, I mistook your glove as a weapon and took the shot to protect myself."

"Wow. You really are delusional."

She tries to get to her feet, but with her hands cuffed behind her back, she fails and lands back on her rear.

"Settle down," Lucas says to us both. "This isn't helping anything. Hawthorne, you, of all people, know that I can't just let you get away with this."

"Trespassing? You could just cite me for trespassing."

To my surprise, Lucas seems to be considering it.

"You can't be serious. She came here to kill you."

"No I didn't."

"Why did you come then?" I ask.

"Why did you?" She counters.

"I'm not the one breaking the law."

"You were not invited, but here you are."

I don't have an answer and I don't owe her one.

"Okay," Lucas snaps. "Stop fighting. Hawthorne, I can't let you go with just a trespass citation. Not when you had a gun. It's pretty clear I have to take you in and let the court decide what to do with you." Lightning illuminates her face and she looks stricken.

She waits on the thunder, then says, "You know what they do to cops in jail."

"You should have thought about that before you came here with a gun," I say.

"Look," she begs, climbing to her knees. "I'm not well. Truly, I'm not. I've had a rough night. Please don't put me in jail. I know I shouldn't have come here, but really, what happened? No one got hurt. I have severe PTSD and tonight it got away from me. Don't ruin my life for a stupid mistake."

There's not a hint of flirting, of coercion. She seems completely earnest in her plea.

I'm moved by her emotion and look at Lucas for his reaction. He's looking back for mine.

She sees us wavering and presses on. "I can go stay with my Great Aunt Pauline and get help. I will take a leave of absence until I get better. Please."

Lucas raises his eyebrows in question. I nod slightly.

He slowly walks behind her and unlocks the cuffs. She rubs at her wrists and thanks him profusely.

"Go straight to your Aunt's. I'm keeping the gun you brought, but I don't want you going home where you have a bunch more available."

"I will. I promise. I'll go right now."

"Mrs. Mott can keep an eye on you. If you step out of line again, even a little, I'll press charges. Do you understand?"

"Wait, Mrs. Mott is your aunt?"

Kalissta nods. "She's the one that helped me get hired on here. She's my grandma's sister."

"Small world," I mutter, not sure how I feel about sending someone with such obvious issues to stay with someone I care about. Of course, Mrs. Mott can take care of herself and care of anyone else that needs it. "You will behave for her, won't you?"

Kalissta spins so fast, water flies from the ends of her hair. "Behave?"

"I mean, you won't give her any trouble."

"Don't pretend you care about her more than I do. Aunt Pauline has been the one person to always believe in me."

"She's always believed in me, too," I counter.

"Well, she's not perfect, then. Is she?" Before we can stop her, Kalissta hurries around the corner of the house and disappears into the rain.

I stare open mouthed at Lucas. He laughs at my expression.

"She has a mouth on her," he says. "Reminds me of someone else I know."

I smack him on the shoulder and the mood instantly changes. The storm is tapering off, but the air sizzles between us. "I still don't know why you are here," he says, meeting my eyes and stepping closer.

Just then, the power comes back on and the light over the sink in the kitchen pours out the patio doors. The sudden light seems bright after the darkness of the storm. It illuminates the bright blue of his eyes and the fire that burns in them.

"Do you really want to know?" I ask, my whole world hanging on his answer.

He steps even closer, close enough I can feel his warm breath on my rain-chilled skin. "I hope God told you to come."

The perfect answer.

"He did," I say breathlessly.

"I didn't understand before." He reaches up and tucks a wet curl behind my ear. "I didn't believe as strongly as I should have. But all that is different now."

"Different how? I'm still going to get messages. I'm still going to do what God says."

"I want you to. See, something has been happening to me the last few days. God has been talking to me. Not the way the talks to you, but in my heart."

"Really?" My heart begins to race, I want to believe him so badly.

"Earlier, after I saw you at the park and screwed that up so immensely, I went to where Crystal is buried. You know that little church there? I went inside and God talked to me." He swallows hard and his voice breaks. "I

112

gave myself to Him. I gave him all that I have and all that I am. It was the most amazing thing. I finally understand what it must be like for you. Actually, I don't, but I'm starting to. I'm kind of jealous of you. Having that kind of relationship with Him."

I reach out and touch his face, run my bare left palm down his wet cheek. As usual, I don't get a vision, but I feel the love just the same.

"It's not easy," I point out.

"No, but you make it look easy." He locks eyes with me and lightening illuminates his face. "Gabby, I love you. That's all that matters now. I love you and need you."

The thunder crashes at the end of his words.

Go to him.

I don't need to be told twice.

I reach my lips to his and he bends to kiss me. His lips are wet, and warm, and not a dream. He pulls my hips against him and I sink into his embrace.

"What does God say now?" he asks after the kiss.

"Do you need to ask?" I lean into him again and our kisses deepen. His hands roam under my jacket and find my skin. His skin is wet and hot, his fingers searching.

"I think I should call Dustin," he says against my ear.

I don't want to think about my brother right now and resent the intrusion. "Why's that?"

"Because he's coming over and I don't want him to right now."

I'd forgotten that we called him. I'd forgotten about Kalissta. I'd forgotten everything except for Lucas.

"What are you going to tell him?"

113

"That I'll explain in the morning. I have other things on my mind right now." He smiles a mischievous grin and sends the text.

He doesn't wait for a response, just takes my hand. "Let's get out of this rain."

I quickly follow him into the house. I peel off my wet jacket, kick off my drenched shoes. He kisses me again, then gets us towels from the hall closet.

I dry my hair as he pulls at my sweater.

I soon give up trying to dry off and let him lead me down the hall.

Once in his bedroom, he switches on the lamp. My necklace glitters from where it hangs. "I believe this is yours," he says.

I touch my empty neck. "I've missed it."

He places the necklace around my neck, reaches behind me and clasps it. "I want to see you wearing nothing but this," he whispers near my ear.

I'm only too happy to comply.

When I wake in Lucas's arms a few hours later, I first think I'm dreaming again. He stirs and the hair on his chest bristles against my cheek. This is no dream. We are together again.

"Is it morning already?" he asks, lazily.

The sun is shining in the bedroom window and onto the bed, "Unfortunately."

He stretches and rolls over to throw his arm across my waist. "Let's just stay here all day."

"I wish. But don't you have to work?"

He groans. "Don't remind me." He nuzzles my neck. "Maybe it can wait?"

His phone buzzes and he groans again. I reach for his phone and see it's from Dustin. I expect it will be him demanding answers from last night.

Instead, the text says, "We have another murder."

Chapter 16

GABBY

Tossing on clothes and rushing out the door before we've even had coffee is not the way I pictured my first morning back together with Lucas. Alexis's many warnings about life with a detective ring in my ears. Poor Alexis. I get to go with Lucas. She's left at home with a toddler.

I should check on her.

I file that thought away for later and hurry to Lucas's car.

His face is pinched with worry as we make our way to the crime scene. He's unusually quiet.

"Is everything okay?" I ask, thinking maybe he regrets last night. Maybe he wishes I'd stayed behind and is too polite to tell me.

He looks my way. "Not really. The address Dustin texted us, I'm pretty sure it's Kalissta's address."

My stomach sinks. "You don't think it's her, do you?"

"Dustin would have told us if she was the victim. I'm more afraid that she did something horrible after we let her go. I knew better than to take pity on her."

I chew on the tip of a finger of my glove, a ball of nerves.

"What are we going to tell Dustin? That we let a possible murderer loose after she shot at me?"

He grips the steering wheel and sighs. "Let's just wait and see what the situation is once we get there."

I don't like waiting. I don't have my phone, or I'd call Mrs. Mott. I don't know her number by heart. I do know Grandma Dot's.

I call her from Lucas's phone. She's curious why I need Mrs. Mott at eight in the morning, but thankfully doesn't press the issue.

A few moments later, Mrs. Mott answers with a curious, "Hello?"

"Mrs. Mott, this is Gabby."

"Gabby, dear. I thought you might call this morning. Are you checking on Kalissta?"

"So she's there?"

"Showed up in the middle of the night, wet and upset. We had some hot tea and a long talk about what she did. She feels terrible. I'm so sorry, she's had some troubles in the past, but never anything like this."

"What time did she get there?"

"It was 2:17 am. I remember because I wondered who in the world was beating on the door at that time. I was worried it might be that crazy ex of hers come looking for her. He's the main reason I had her move here. Randy wouldn't leave her alone, regardless of the restraining order."

"She got there about ten minutes after she left us," I

tell Lucas with obvious relief.

"Gabby, what's going on?" Mrs. Mott asks.

"I can't talk about it yet," I hedge.

"Oh no. I know what that means." Mrs. Mott doesn't miss much. "Does it involve Kalissta? Oh no. That poor girl has been through so much already. I really thought River Bend would be a fresh start for her."

"Mrs. Mott, please stay calm. And keep Kalissta there. I'm sure everything will be fine," I hope I sound believable.

"You can't fool me, Gabby. You never could. If my niece is in some sort of trouble, you do everything you can to help her. I know you can."

"I will," I say as we approach the house surrounded by crime scene tape. "Mrs. Mott, I'm sorry, but I have to go."

"Wait, you are coming to the party tonight, right? Derek really wants to meet you."

"I'll be there." I hang up before she can respond. "Is that her house?" I ask Lucas.

"Yeah. It is."

I'm happy to see that the Coroner's van is not here yet, so I don't have to deal with Gomez. Officer Patterson is out front, guarding the tape. Dustin is standing in front of the open garage door talking to another uniformed officer. A brown UPS delivery truck is parked in front of the house just outside of the tape. The driver leans against it, waiting.

"Wonder what that's about," I say to Lucas as we duck under the tape. Officer Patterson sees us together and smiles brightly. "Detective Hartley," he says formally, then adds with a twinkle, "Gabby, good morning."

My liking of the officer deepens. He's always had my back.

Dustin turns as we approach, a flicker of surprise crosses his eyes when he sees us together. "Good," he says looking from me to Lucas. That's all he has to say on the subject of us being together this morning, an obvious sign we kissed and made up. "We have a doozy here," he continues.

I peek into the garage and quickly turn away. There's a man on the floor, a large pool of blood surrounding him. So much blood it's seeped under the door and out onto the driveway. It's obvious he has been stabbed several times. I've seen many murder victims, this one is brutal.

I put my hand to my mouth and turn away from the grisly scene.

"The UPS guy came this morning with an early morning next-day-air delivery. When he walked past the garage, he saw this seeping out of the door. He says he's a hunter and recognized it as drying blood."

I look across the yard at the poor delivery driver. He sees me watching him and looks away, uncomfortable.

"He called 911 and Officer Shipman here was the first on scene. Shipman, this is Gabby McAllister, a consultant for us."

I nearly fall down in shock. Dustin has never called me a consultant before. Shipman reaches to shake my hand, sees my gloves, makes the connection of who I am and drops his hand. He says hello friendly enough, though, so I don't hold it against him.

"You know this is Kalissta Hawthorne's house," Lucas says softly. "She called me last night to come over. She thought someone was trying to break in. I didn't see anyone when I got here."

I school my face into a neutral expression. I had no idea Lucas was here last night. I wonder what happened that upset Kalissta so badly that she came to his house with a gun. Lucas brushes his fingers across mine, a tiny touch to let me know we're okay.

It doesn't matter what he did before, he spent the night with me. Will spend all his nights with me, now.

"Do we know who the victim is?" I ask.

Dustin hands Lucas an ID. "This was in his wallet. She didn't bother to take it out."

"Randy Benson," Lucas reads.

"Did you say Randy?"

He shows me the ID. "Yeah, why?"

"Mrs. Mott just mentioned a Randy in connection with Kalissta. Said she had a crazy ex that was bothering her. She even had a restraining order against him."

The four of us exchange looks. "This doesn't look good," Lucas says. "But I can't imagine her doing that." He motions to the body on the floor.

"Yeah, me either," Dustin says. "But we've seen crazy stuff before. Did you see all the weapons in her house? Something's not quite right there." He looks at me. "Do you want to try to see something before Gomez gets here? We only have a few minutes."

I really don't. I don't even want to look at what was once Randy Benson. I don't want to think that a woman I

121

know did that to another person. I don't want to live through his death.

I go cold and take a step back. "Do I have to?"

"No. She doesn't." Lucas comes to my defense.

Officer Shipman looks uncomfortable. Dustin looks confused. He glances into the garage then at me. "Yeah, maybe I don't blame you."

"I can at least see what he's doing here, maybe. He lives in South Bend. Why is he so far from home?" I step to the front porch, sit down and take off my gloves.

"You ready?" Lucas asks. I appreciate the concern, but am ready to do my work. I nod and say my prayer and then reach for the driver's license.

The vision is fuzzy and I don't get any clear words or sights. What I do get is an obsession, fear and pain and dark death.

I toss the ID away before I get any more of the murder. I open my eyes and find everyone, even the UPS guy, watching me.

"I'm sorry, I didn't get anything other than an obsession feeling. Then I started feeling the murder and I stopped the vision."

"I didn't know you could stop them," Dustin says, interested.

"I didn't either, but I really don't want to live through that. If I had to guess, he was here stalking Kalissta the way he did back in South Bend. That's kind of obvious, though. Why else would he be here?"

The rough wood of the steps is pushing into the backs of my thighs and the morning sun is glaring into my eyes.

I'm starting to feel like a bug on display with the men staring at me, so I stand. "Sorry," I say lamely, brushing off my rear and handing back the ID.

Patterson has wandered over. "Don't worry, Gabby. We all know you're amazing."

I don't feel amazing, but give Patterson a smile anyway. "Thanks."

I look around for anything else I can do before Gomez arrives and I'm kicked out. I feel the UPS guy watching me with open interest. "You keeping him around for a reason?" I ask Dustin.

"He hasn't given his full statement yet. He already called into the center and they are sending someone to relieve him."

"What was he bringing to Kalissta?"

"He said and early a.m. next-day-air package."

"Do you think that's weird?"

Dustin shrugs. "Who knows?"

"When's the last time you got an early a.m. next-day-air package? That sounds important."

I walk towards the UPS driver and he stiffens. "Hey," he says. "That was pretty impressive over there."

"Not really," I say. "Normally, I see more." I sense Lucas behind me. "Can I see the package that you were to deliver this morning?"

The driver takes a small box from the steps leading into his truck. When he hands it to me, it sizzles through the cardboard into my bare fingertips.

I drop the package on the ground.

"What's wrong?" Lucas asks.

"There's something in the box."

Chapter 17

GABBY

Lucas bends and picks the box up off the grass. He gives it a shake and something rattles inside.

"Mind if I open it?" he asks the driver.

"Just sign for it and it's yours." He holds out a computerized board and Lucas signs for the package.

"Do you have a knife or something to cut the tape?"

The driver climbs the steps into his truck and returns a moment later with a box knife. "Will this work?"

Lucas takes the knife as Dustin, Shipman and Patterson join us. "Gabby says something important is in this box." He opens the knife and slits the tape.

We all lean closer as the box opens. Inside is a medal on a blue ribbon. Lucas pulls it out with the tip of the knife. "Looks like a marksman medal. The kind we got in the academy."

"What does that mean? Hawthorne finished academy a few years ago. Besides, they give those out in person, not by UPS," Dustin says.

All the men look at me.

"What?" I ask, although I know what they want.

Lucas says, "Only if you want to."

"Fine." I take a breath and lean against the side of the UPS truck to keep me steady. "Lord, let me see what I need to see," I say and reach for the medal.

This vision is harsh and powerful.

Mine. My girl. Hands put the medal around a neck. Auburn hair flows around it. Pride mixes with desire and possession.

Lucas shakes me out of the vision.

"What?" I say, blinking back to reality. I'm sitting on the curb, leaning against the tire of the UPS truck.

"You were moaning and your legs went out. I didn't like it."

"A desire pumped through me, stronger than I've ever felt before. It makes poor Randy Benson's obsession pale in comparison." I struggle to breathe. "Whoever sent this to Kalissta knew her. They presented the medal to her. Is there a return address?"

Lucas looks at the box, then helps me to my feet. "There isn't one on the box. Do you have one?"

The driver checks his board, "It shows the UPS Store here in River Bend."

"That isn't too helpful. But maybe they have records or at least a video or something we can go on," Dustin says.

"Do you think whoever sent this has something to do with the murder?" Patterson asks me.

I'm surprised to be asked my opinion. "I don't know for sure, but it is a bit coincidental that the body is found the same morning that Kalissta gets this package."

"Do you think Kalissta killed Randy?" Dustin asks me. I about slide to the ground again that Dustin is asking my opinion.

I think about my answer. "She wasn't here last night. I mean, she could have done it before she went to Lucas's house, but she was pretty intent on him last night. I don't see her doing that," I wave toward the garage, "then going to Lucas's the way she did."

"I don't think she'd call me over if she had just brutally killed her ex and stashed him in her garage. She's a bit disturbed, but I don't think she's that crazy."

Patterson and Shipman exchange glances at mention of Lucas being there last night. I glare at the two men. Patterson catches my look and drops his eyes to the ground.

"So, if Kalissta didn't do it, then whoever sent her this medal must have," I point out.

Dustin carefully puts the medal into an evidence bag.

"How did they get the medal? If they gave it to her, like I saw, how did they have it to send?"

No one has an answer to that.

"Maybe they stole it?" Lucas offers. "Let's go check the house. She has a lot of things on display. Maybe she has her medals and this one is missing."

"Is there a way to find out who gave it to her in the first place?" I ask. "They seemed very obsessed with her. Maybe that's who stole it and sent it to her." I lower my voice. "And who killed Randy."

"We're definitely going to look into it," Dustin says, then looks behind me. His shoulders drop. "Gomez is here. You better take off."

I resist the urge to look over my shoulder. The longer

Gomez doesn't see my face, the better.

"What can I do to help?" I ask quickly. "I can go to the UPS Store."

"You will not. That is our job," Lucas says, softly, but firmly, with a slight edge. "And don't even think of talking to Kalissta. We will do that, too."

The coroner van pulls up behind the UPS truck. I feel Gomez glaring at me. "Uh, I better go."

I walk around the front of the brown truck as Lucas hands me his keys. I wish I could kiss him goodbye, but settle for sneaking away.

My pride is bruised as I drive away from the crime scene. I'm not a criminal and it hurts to be treated like one. Or like a child being sent home. I have wracked my brain to find a way to win Gomez over to my side, but nothing that might work has come to mind.

I'm still seething as I let myself into my front door. I'm so preoccupied, it takes a moment to realize the door is unlocked.

I push against the peeling paint and open the door a crack, "Hello?"

Chester darts out the crack and I nearly stumble off the steps in surprise.

My first thought is that my father has returned. He's snuck into my house before.

But he's tucked away in jail and I've changed my locks since then just to be safe.

I take off my left glove and touch the door knob. I get a jolt of the same energy I got from the medal. An obsessive desire.

Someone's been here. Someone who knows how to unlock a door without a key.

"You okay?" Preston calls from his driveway, making me jump.

Preston, again. After months of not talking, he's suddenly everywhere.

Or just dragging his trash can in.

"I'm fine. Hey, did you see anyone around here last night?"

He looks from Lucas's car, then to me, a question in his eyes. I can see him make the connection that I didn't spend last night home alone. Even after what he said at the fire.

"No," he says shortly, then turns and re-enters his house.

I'm left by myself with the open door. I quickly push it all the way open, half-expecting someone to jump out at me.

There, in bright red letters, spray-painted on the living room wall, are the words. "Come find me."

I step backward on the steps and my foot slides off. I stumble and fall into the grass. The words are huge and angry looking.

They seem to mock me.

Chester pounces on my lap and I make a startled noise. I wish Preston would come back out. I search the neighborhood, but I'm alone.

I left my phone by the table inside the door last night. I reach around the door jamb and snag it, ready to call Lucas. I hesitate over the call button. He has his hands full with the Randy Benson murder. My break-in can wait.

But there's no way I'm going into my house now. Not until the police come and check it out.

Using just the tips of my fingers, I pull the door shut tight and back away from the house.

"Who wants me to come find them?"

The same person that brutally murdered Randy Benson. I do want to find that person. Want to find them and lock them up.

Or worse.

Chapter 18

I watch her as she falls off the front steps and lands in the grass. She must have seen the message I left for her.

I know she saw what I left for Kalissta. I wonder what she thought.

Was she impressed?

Did she touch the body and see my work firsthand?

Does she understand yet?

What a lovely distraction she has been.

But my true work now begins.

Chapter 19

GABBY

My blood is pumping as I drive to Lucas's to switch cars.

Someone was in my house.

Someone scared Chester.

He's fine now. I collected him from the yard and he sits on my lap as I drive. I pet him between the ears, wishing he could talk, could tell me who broke into the house.

I feel a little better once I'm back in my Charger. Chester settles on the passenger seat and looks up at me as if to say, "Now what?"

"Good question." I put the car into drive and head where I always head.

Grandma Dot's. If nothing else, I can't investigate with Chester. He will be safe at Grandma Dot's.

I'm happy to see Mom's car by the barn. I also notice Mrs. Mott's car. For a moment, I think about turning around and leaving. If Mrs. Mott is here, then Kalissta may be, too.

Holding Chester close to my chest, I enter the kitchen.

Jet wriggles through the crack of the sliding door to the

beauty shop. He puts his front paws on my leg and sniffs at Chester.

Chester digs his claws into my skin. I hurry upstairs with the cat and put him down on the bed in my old, yellow, room. He hisses at Jet.

"Leave him alone," I say and shoo the dog out the door.

Grandma Dot looks up from Mrs. Mott's freshly purpled poof when I enter the beauty shop. "I thought that was your car I heard roar in here a few minutes ago." She pats Mrs. Mott's hair. I search the shop for Kalissta.

"She's not here," Mrs. Mott says. "The police took her in to question. That detective of yours and your brother wouldn't tell me what was going on. I came here to find out from you what they want with my niece."

"You also had an appointment for this morning," Grandma points out, taking the cape from Mrs. Mott's neck.

"Well, that's beside the point. I may just cancel the whole party tonight. I mean, Kalissta being questioned? What is wrong with this world?" Mrs. Mott's hair bobs as she stands and faces me. "Spill it, girlie."

"Now, Mrs. Mott," Mom pipes in. "Don't put Gabby on the spot like that. If she can talk to us, she will."

Mrs. Mott pushes her lips together and stares me down.

"You won't like it," I hedge.

"I already don't like it," she counters.

"I guess it will be all over town soon enough. Plus, I know Kalissta didn't do it."

"Gabriella," Grandma says seriously. "What's going

on?"

"A man was found brutally murdered in Kalissta's garage this morning. It is that crazy ex you told me about, Randy Benson."

The three women gasp.

"She didn't do it. I know she didn't," Mrs. Mott says.

"I know that, too. Whoever killed Randy also broke into my house and wrote on my wall. Kalissta was home with you by then."

"That's right. We stayed up talking and sipping tea after she arrived. We talked well into the early morning."

"You don't have to convince me. I'm sure it will get figured out once they question her."

"They sure will. Oh, poor Kalissta."

"I'm sure it will all work out," Mom says.

"There's more you're not telling," Grandma says fingering her neck. I reach for the necklace back in its rightful place on me. I feel my face burn.

"Yeah. Lucas and I made up last night. Turns out being shot at really puts things in perspective relationship-wise." I look away from Grandma's prying eyes.

"Good for you," Mom gushes. "I knew you two would figure it out."

Mrs. Mott is staring at me. "What do you mean being shot at? Kalissta didn't tell me that part."

Of course she didn't.

"She kind of had a gun and shot at me. She missed, then Lucas tackled her."

"Oh, no," Mrs. Mott gasps again. "She certainly didn't tell me about a gun. Oh that girl was in a state last night.

She has suffered since she was discharged from the Army. She doesn't talk about her time overseas. She just tells me she saw some things that changed her."

"Poor thing," Mom says.

"A lot of the soldiers where changed. I've tried to help her. She ran into trouble back in South Bend. Missed too many days or something is what she said. Now I wonder."

"Don't wonder too hard," Grandma says. "Just trust her."

"I thought I did the right thing helping her get the job on the force here. Maybe it's all been too much." I've never seen Mrs. Mott so shook up.

"She's going to be fine," Grandma says sternly. "She'll talk to the boys and this will all get figured out. Now stop worrying about what you can't control. Let's talk about the party tonight. Do you know what you're going to wear?"

Mrs. Mott lets herself be distracted. I sit down on one of the chairs, half-listening to them talk, half-debating with myself about what I should do next. As usual, I'm left out of the actual investigation. Dustin had called me a consultant. I wonder how that's different than the outsider I've always been. Can I get an assignment like that?

It would sure be nice to not slink away when Gomez shows up. Nice to be there talking to Kalissta or processing the scene.

I turn my thoughts to the information I do know. The medal. Someone sent it to her. The same man that gave it to her.

"Mrs. Mott," I interrupt suddenly. "Were you there when Kalissta graduated from the academy?"

"I sure was. We were so proud of her."

"Do you know who presented her with the marksmanship medal?" I ask hopefully.

"Oh it was lovely. Her favorite instructor, Officer Janet Stapleton presented it to her. I think I saw a tear in her eye."

"Janet? A woman?" I ask, crestfallen. I'd been sure the vision I saw was from a man. A very obsessed man.

"Yes, a woman. You know women can be police instructors, too."

"I know. That's not what I mean."

Mrs. Mott studies my face. "How did you know she was presented with a marksmanship medal?"

I press my lips together. Divulging that a body was found is one thing. Giving away intimate details of the case is another. "I can't-."

"You can't tell us. I see. Really, Gabby you should be a cop, too. You sure guard information like one."

I see Grandma's face light up. "You should," she says, full of enthusiasm.

"Yes, what a great idea," Mom adds.

"Oh, come on. Don't you think we have enough cops in this family already?"

"Is there such a thing?" Grandma says. "Gabriella as a cop. I like it."

Mrs. Mott seems pleased with herself.

"I'll think about it," I say to shut them up. I need to escape.

Grandma kisses me goodbye. "Seriously. Think about it," she says near my ear.

I resist rolling my eyes, because I know Grandma won't like it. "I've got to go do some stuff." I kiss Mom on the cheek.

"You are coming to my party tonight still, right?" Mrs. Mott says.

"Yes, you are coming," Mom says.

"I'll come. I said I would." I'm tired of hearing about the party and slide the door to the kitchen. "Chester is upstairs in my old room."

"Why's that?"

"He was scared after the break-in."

"Break-in. I thought that's what you said earlier, but you didn't bring it up again and I thought I must have heard you wrong," Grandma says, following me into the kitchen, Mom and Mrs. Mott right behind her.

"Was anything taken?" Mom asks.

"Not taken, but he left something. A message on my wall in spray-paint. It said 'come find me'."

"What does that mean?" Mom exclaims.

"It means that whoever has been killing people and making it look like suicide killed Randy Benson last night and knows I'm involved."

Grandma steps forward. "Stay here. You can't go out if someone is after you like that."

"I can't sit here while someone targets me. I have to find out who is behind all this."

"If you were a cop, you'd at least have a gun," Grandma pushes.

"Okay, okay. That's enough with the cop talk. I already have a killer to track."

138

"I don't like this," Mom says taking my hand. I get the feeling she wants to hold onto my hand and not let go.

"I'll be okay," I say, pulling from her grasp. "I always am."

I hurry out of the kitchen, saying over my shoulder. "Give Chester some food and water, please. I'll see you tonight."

Chapter 20

GABBY

On the road back to River Bend, I think about the idea of becoming a cop. I would have access to cases, which would be nice. But I'd start out on patrol and I don't see how that would work.

Still, the idea has some merit. I don't know what will happen with the shop now and being an officer would be a steady job.

It wouldn't give me the access I need. Like now. Lucas and Dustin are interviewing Kalissta right now. I'm stuck on the outside. As a patrol, I'd be out of the interview room, too. How I want to be a part of that interview.

Consultant. Dustin had called me a consultant. If I really was a consultant, I could be there right now finding out firsthand what she has to say about Randy and who might be trying to frame her.

Or at least scare her.

They certainly have scared me. I don't want to go back to my house. I could go touch the letters scrawled on my wall, but I truly don't want to. If the killer is the one who etched them there, and I have no doubt he is, I don't want to crawl into his head again. I don't want to see what he has in that mind about me.

Why is he after me at all?

If this is about Kalissta, why include me?

So many questions and no answers.

I park in the alley of my shop and take out my keys to unlock the door. When I slide the key into the lock, for a moment, I think this door is unlocked, too. That someone has broken in to the shop.

I freeze and wipe sudden sweat off my forehead. Mom sleeps here. If someone broke in while she was here....

I try the key again and realize I was wrong. The door is locked.

I push it open carefully just the same. I duck my head inside, half expecting another message on the wall. The shop is quiet. Eerily quiet. Dust dances in the beam of sunshine coming in the front window, the word "Messages" in a fancy script in shadow on the wooden floor.

Spinning a slow circle, everything looks to be in place. No angry red words, no madman.

It suddenly strikes me that being alone in the shop may not be a good idea. There's a killer on the loose and he has targeted me.

"Come find me," he'd said.

"I will find you."

Sitting at the front counter that also serves as my desk, I open my laptop and type in the name Kalissta Hawthorne and add South Bend, Indiana.

Besides a Facebook page and a twitter account that it looks like she hasn't posted to in months, I only find a small mention of her. It's an article about the new recruits

142

graduating from the academy. Her name is listed with about two dozen others. I scan the list, but nothing jumps out at me.

I spend the next half hour poking around the internet, reading her Facebook page and trying to get a feel for why this woman is involved in something so horrendous as the murder.

For my trouble, I don't find anything useful.

I sit back in my chair and watch a couple walk by my door and down the sidewalk. They are holding hands and talking close. It makes me miss Lucas.

I take out my phone and send him a quick text. "You still interviewing Kalissta?"

A few minutes later, when he hasn't gotten back to me, I pick my phone up again. This time I text my friend Haley. She's a whiz with the computer and has done some hacking for me on occasion.

"You up for a little digging around?"

The response is immediate. "Always. What you got?"

I text her the info I have on Kalissta and ask her to look into her life, especially her time at the academy. Whoever is behind this sent her a medal from there. It has to be the link.

Haley assures me she'll work on it right away.

So I wait.

Since my computer is open, I check my bank account. I don't like what I see so I close the computer.

I straighten the papers on my desk, organize my pens, wipe up an old coffee stain.

The waiting is driving me crazy.

When the phone finally rings, I jump and snatch the phone off my desk. It's not Haley, it's not even Lucas.

It's Lacey Aniston. I press answer and say, "Hello?"

"Hey Gabby, just checking in."

I scrunch my face in disbelief. Why would Lacey feel she needed to check in?

"I'm okay," I hedge.

"Well, I heard about this morning at the cop's house. I figured you were there." She leaves the sentence hanging.

I don't take the bait.

"You know I can't tell you anything."

"But you probably told your Grandma."

She has me there. It irks me that she knows me so well.

"That's different. Grandma can keep the info to herself, not blast it on the news."

"But this is important. If there really is a serial killer out cutting people up, the public deserves to know about it."

"Then ask Lucas and Dustin. I can't give you a statement. I'm sorry."

She sighs heavily and I brace for her retort.

"I suppose you're right." I'm shocked that she let me win so easily. Since our adventure together we have become friendly, but I've never known Lacey to back down. "You still going to Mrs. Mott's party tonight?"

That darn party. I truly don't feel like going. "I promised to go, so yes."

"Are we still driving together?"

So she can pump me for information. "I suppose, if you want."

"Great. I'll drive. I can pick you up in a few hours."

I don't want to go home, but I'm still wearing the clothes I tossed on last night. Grandma would not like it if I showed up in this outfit. "Okay. I'll be ready."

I get another call and see it's Haley. I hurry to get Lacey off the phone and say "What you got?"

"That's a way to say hello," Haley laughs. "You just waiting by the phone for me to call back?"

"Maybe," I laugh. I've missed Haley. We used to work together, but now rarely see each other. Our relationship has dwindled down to a few sporadic texts. "Sorry, I just get excited."

"That's what I like about you. Now onto the mysterious Kalissta."

"Did you find anything useful?"

"Not that I can see. I have her records from the academy. Mostly her grades and reports from instructors. Nothing of note, really. She did well, I can see that. No misconduct or anything that was noted in her file."

I run my finger along the edge of my desk, listening, disappointed. I'd really thought something about the academy was behind all this. Why else send the medal?

"I also found a restraining order against a Randy Benson. That angle might lead to somewhere."

"It already has," I say. "Randy Benson was murdered last night."

"Really?" Haley gasps. "Poor thing. Of course, from the report with the restraining order, he didn't sound like a very nice guy. He tossed her around some, then wouldn't stop following her. There was a more recent report, from

145

just a few months ago of him standing outside her house, watching her. She called 911, but there was nothing they could do. It was a public road and he was just outside the perimeter of the order."

"Poor Kalissta."

"Yeah, he wasn't the nicest guy, but to be murdered?"

She has no idea that he wasn't just murdered, he was brutalized.

"You sure she didn't do it?" Haley asks. "I can see how that would drive a woman to kill a man."

"It wasn't her."

"So why the deep dive into her background?"

"She's the key, somehow. The body was found in her garage."

"Sounds like she did it. I'm sure you have your reasons for saying she's innocent, but it smells fishy to me."

"The whole thing smells fishy. Is there anything else? Even a little detail might help me."

"Nothing interesting. For fun, I broke into her Facebook account and poked around. The usual posts and pictures. She did have some photos that she deleted from her page. I found that interesting, so I recovered them."

"You can do that?"

She makes a small sound of disbelief, "Of course. It's not even that hard. Anyway the pics are of her and some guy. Probably that Randy guy. If she was having issues like that, she most likely wanted to erase him from her life."

"Thanks, Haley. Can you send me the pictures? I'll see if they are of Randy or who's in them. Send me the files from the academy, too and anything else you have."

"Can do."

"You're the best."

"How's that handsome detective of yours? You guys still hot and heavy?"

I'm glad I can say we are. "Doing good." I leave out the part about the last week. It's in the past and I want to leave it there.

"I'm glad. He's good for you. We should get together once you solve this case."

"I'd like that," I say sincerely. "I really would."

"Maybe we can double date. I met someone." Haley tells me all about her latest boyfriend. He's the fifth since I've known her. Each one is Mr. Wonderful for a few weeks, then she passes him on and goes hunting for the next.

"A double date sounds great. Just after we put this serial killer away."

"Serial killer? You didn't say this was that kind of case. Should I be worried?"

"No. His MO is to go after those that have had a shady past. It's almost like he's trying to clean up the streets. Of course, he's doing it the wrong way."

"A little hacking doesn't count as a shady past, does it?" she asks, only half joking.

"Don't worry. We'll catch the guy."

"How many has he killed? Gosh, this is scary."

"We don't really know. He made them look like suicides. Until last night."

"What made last night different?"

"That's what I'm trying to figure out."

Chapter 21

DUSTIN

Although little surprises me in this job anymore, I find it hard to believe that the woman across the table from us is capable of stabbing and cutting Randy Benson so brutally, let alone the other murders we think are done by the same person. In all my dealings with her as an officer, Kalissta Hawthorne has been the epitome of professionalism. Always eager to please, very respectful.

Of course, she's also the same woman that took a gun to Lucas's and shot at Gabby. Hard to picture that from her either.

We don't get much more information than we had before. She had no idea how Randy ended up in her garage. Didn't even know he was in town. The last time she saw her medal, it was hanging with her other medals in her bedroom. She didn't realize it was gone and has no idea who would UPS it to her.

Basically, if Hawthorne knows anything, she's not talking.

Since we don't have anything concrete to hold her on and her alibi is Lucas and Mrs. Mott, we have to let her go.

When the interview is over, she stands and offers her

hand for us to shake. I shake it, but Lucas looks away. He's been unusually quiet the whole time we've been talking with her. Understandable after the mess with her last night.

"You know the drill," I tell her. "Don't leave town or anything."

"I'm hoping to get back to work. Today is my day off, but I'm scheduled back tomorrow. Do you think this will interfere with working?" She nibbles on her bottom lip and looks sincerely concerned about her job.

"That's not up to us," Lucas says. "You need to talk to the chief."

She bobs her head, "Right. I'll do that."

I show her out the door, say goodbye, and head for our office. My chair squeaks as I sit.   I find the coffee with extra cream and sugar I treated myself to and take a sip. It's cold. I put the cup down too hard and coffee sloshes onto the desk.

"Man," I say, wiping the stain with a stray napkin tucked into my top drawer next to some stale candy.

Lucas digs in his drawer and finds a crumpled paper towel. He tosses it to me and I finish cleaning up my mess. "Well, that interview was useless," Lucas says taking his seat opposite me. "Either she is clueless as she says or she's covering for someone."

"I don't think she'd do that. Not for a person who's killed at least three people. And those are just the ones Gabby's confirmed."

"She did seem genuinely surprised when we showed up at Mrs. Mott's this morning."

"And upset about Randy, even though he wasn't her favorite person," I add.

"Again, she could be faking it. She was certainly unstable last night."

I try sipping my cold coffee and look at him over the rim. "Speaking of last night, I couldn't help but notice you and Gabby came to the scene together this morning. Can I assume that means you two kissed and made up?"

His cheeks turn a slight shade of pink behind his stubble. "Yeah, we got things figured out."

"Good." I sit my cup down without spilling it. "So where do you want to go next?"

"Check out the UPS store I guess. They should have cameras. Couldn't be too many people that sent an early a.m. package. Why send it like that? It has to mean something to Kalissta."

"If it does she's not talking." I stand and grab the keys to the cruiser. As I do, my stomach growls loudly. "I'll check out the UPS store. You talk to the crime scene crew and see if they found anything while we were in interview."

Lucas picks up the phone as I leave. "Think I'll call the academy too and see what I can find out about the medal and her time there. There has to be some connection she either isn't telling us about or we just aren't seeing yet."

"You know who's good at seeing," I say.

Lucas smiles. "I'll check with her, too. She texted me a bit ago. I'll see if she found out anything. She usually does."

"You just want to talk to her."

151

"Can you blame me? It's been a long week."

My stomach grumbles again as I drive towards the UPS store. I'm not in the mood for fast food. What I really want is more of the meatloaf Alexis made for dinner last night and I had to eat reheated.

I make a turn and take a detour to my house. It's really not too far from the downtown square where the UPS store is. Besides, a man has to eat.

I park in the driveway since I'm in a cruiser, not my car and don't have my garage door opener.

As I walk up the sidewalk, a tingle of adrenaline blooms in my belly. Alexis was irritated with me after the middle of the night call from Lucas that ended with me turning around and coming back to bed. This morning's call from dispatch didn't make her mood any better. At least I can spend a few moments with Walker. He's growing so fast and I feel like I'm missing it.

I let myself in the front door, expecting to hear the TV or see Alexis in the kitchen making Walker's lunch.

The house is so quiet, I can hear the sound machine playing a babbling brook coming from Walker's room. "Hello?" I call into the empty house a tingle of nerves snaking up my back. Alexis didn't mention she was going out today.

I cross the kitchen and throw open the door to the garage. Her car is gone.

Slightly concerned, I stare at the empty garage. "Where did you go?"

I dial her number, but it goes directly to voicemail. "Why is your phone off?"

The cop half of me thinks of all the dangers in the world and the what ifs crowd my brain. The husband half of me wonders again why Alexis has been so distant lately. The idea that she might be seeing someone else rears its ugly head for a moment. Then I squash it. She'd never do that. I feel ashamed for even thinking it.

I push the bad thoughts away, realizing I'm overreacting. She probably took Walker to the park or went to the store or any number of innocent things.

Still, the meatloaf sits heavy on my dry tongue as I quickly scarf down some food. I do a quick search of the house before I leave, though I don't know what I expect to find. Everything is in perfect order. Even Walker's toys are put away.

I try her phone again and again it goes straight to voicemail. I think about sending her a text, but she won't get that either if her phone is off. Besides, I don't want her to think I'm checking up on her.

I lock the door behind me and return to my trip to the UPS store. I'll have to worry about Alexis later.

The UPS store is on the same block surrounding the courthouse that Gabby's shop is on. I pull onto the square near the shop and see the Charger in the alley. I think about stopping in and asking Gabby if she found anything useful this morning. Knowing my sister, she's been nosing around the case.

It wouldn't be the first time she's helped us behind the scenes. The idea of making her a consultant like I said this morning flitters through my mind again. It would certainly simplify things.

153

I drive around the square towards the store when my mind stops.

Alexis's car is parked by restaurant on the corner. I'm sure it is her car, but I have no idea why it's here.

I quickly take a spot directly in front of her car and check the sidewalk, searching for my wife.

The only business near here that looks like one she'd visit is a restaurant. Before I can question myself, I climb out of the car and make my way to their door. A few tables sit out on the sidewalk. As always, I draw attention with my uniform and a few patrons look my way. None of them are Alexis.

Inside the restaurant, the hostess looks up with concern. "Is everything okay?" she asks.

I'm used to the reaction, but I suddenly feel silly. "Uh, I'm just looking for someone," I tell her.

The hostess's eyes grow wide.

"No, not like that. I was supposed to meet someone here for lunch."

"Oh," her shoulders relax and a smile touches her lips. "Feel free to look around."

I don't need to go further in. The dining area is small and Alexis is not here.

"On second thought, I think I'll go," I say, wishing I hadn't come in.

The hostess seems confused and her smile grows tight. I hurry back onto the sidewalk. I don't see any other place that Alexis would go to on the block.

Then I hear her laugh and I turn towards the sound. She's coming out of a glass door, talking to another man.

Her head is tilted and she's smiling up at him, laughing at something he said.

My stomach tightens at the sight. I hadn't really expected her to be with another man. That had been a dark, shameful thought. But here she is.

And on the sidewalk for everyone to see.

"Alexis?" I say. "What are you doing here?"

Her face falls when she sees me, and a guilty look crosses her features.

My stomach plummets.

"Dustin, how did you find me?"

"I am here on a case and I saw your car," I say stiffly, looking the other man up and down. He's balding and has a slight belly and stands a few inches shorter than me. I don't see what might attract her to him. "Who's this?" I take a step towards the man. I expect him to bristle, but he steps back and raises a hand to shake mine.

"I'm Larry Jenkins." I don't take his hand. "You must be the husband we've heard about."

Alexis goes stiff. "Larry. Thank you for walking me out," she says, dismissing him.

"Okay, then. I'll see you next time." Larry scurries down the sidewalk.

"How dare you?" Alexis says in a tight voice. "You barely have time for me at home, but here you are following me."

"I'm not following you." Her anger surprises me. I'm the one that should be angry. "But I see I caught you." I flick my eyes at Larry's retreating back.

"Caught me?" she hisses. "Are you serious?"

155

"What other reason do you have for sneaking around down here?" I suddenly realize Walker isn't with her. "Where's my son?"

"*Our* son is at Grandma Dot's. She's been helping me out?" She looks me straight in the eye, "What are *you* doing here? Thought you were on a big case. "

Her gaze is so intense, so upset, I have to look away. "I am on a case. I need to talk to the UPS store over there. I stopped by the house and you weren't there, then I saw your car." It sounds lame, even to me.

"And thought you'd ambush me?"

I don't like the sound of that. "You still haven't told me what you are doing here. What is this place?" I look at the glass doors she came out and see the small church sign. "You going to church here?"

This time, she can't look me in the eyes. "Something like that."

I take her hand in mine, "Look, I know something has been going on the last few months. I think it's time you told me what it is."

Alexis takes a deep breath and raises her eyes. "I've been going to AA meetings here," she says quietly. "That man you just met is my sponsor."

A mixture of relief and surprise and concern washes over me. "AA? As in Alcoholics Anonymous?"

She nods. "I've been coming for a few months."

"I had no idea."

"I didn't want you to know. Look, I'm dealing with it and I've been sober for 93 days. I'm taking care of it."

I squeeze her hand in mine. Her fingers feel small and

156

fragile. An urge to protect her floods through me. "You should have told me. I could have been helping you."

Did I really have no idea or did I just not want to see? Snippets of memory slide into my mind, times when I thought maybe she'd had a little too much wine. I'd ignored the signs. I'd pretended we were okay.

"I couldn't tell you. You are so busy with work all the time, you rarely have time for Walker and me. The drinking started as a way to fill the hours until you were home. As a way to make myself feel good about things again. But it got out of hand."

I feel instantly guilty. "This is because of me?"

She snaps her eyes at me, "No. This is all me. I chose a coward's path before. Now I'm being stronger." She raises her chin.

I take both her hands in mine now. "You are strong. You always have been. You are amazing."

Her hard look softens. "Really?" The hopeful note in her voice tugs at my heart.

"Yes, really." I pull her head onto my chest and she melts into me and wraps her arms around my waist. "I'm so sorry you've been dealing with this alone. I should have been here by your side the whole time."

"You're here now. It is such a relief to finally tell you." She raises her head and her delicious lips are near mine.

"I'll always be by your side, Alexis. I love you." I give into the urge and dip my lips to hers.

When the sweet kiss is over, I raise my head. A few patrons at the restaurant next door are watching us with interest, but I don't care who sees.

"I love you, too," she says breathlessly. "This is such a weight off. I promise, no more secrets."

"None," I agree.

"We'll talk more at home. Now, don't you have a killer to catch?" she teases.

"I do. Are you sure you don't mind that I need to work right now?"

"I'd prefer we were going home, but I understand. Truly, Dustin, I do understand. It just gets hard."

"I know. It's hard not being home, too." I kiss her on the forehead and breathe in the scent of her shampoo. "When we catch this guy, we'll take a vacation. Maybe go to Lake Michigan for a few days. Spend some time, just the three of us."

She looks me in the face and smiles, "I'd like that. Now, you mentioned something about the UPS store."

"Right." I drop my arms from her waist. "Duty calls."

"Go get them, Detective." She tries to sound playful, but it comes out sad.

I'd rather go home with my wife, but I have a job to do. The whole town depends on it. With the taste of her still on my lips, I walk around the block to the UPS store and hopefully to some surveillance footage of the killer.

Chapter 22

KALISSTA HAWTHORNE

Sweat dripped down my sides throughout the entire interview with Lucas and Detective McAllister. I'd hoped to avoid seeing Lucas after last night's humiliation. He's glimpsed a side of me that I've carefully kept hidden.

And then hauled me in for questioning.

I'd told them I was sorry for the loss of Randy, but I'm not. That man made my life hell and the world is a better place without him in it.

But I didn't kill him.

I know I didn't.

I do have a gap in my memory of last night, but as much as I hated Randy Benson, it isn't in me to kill him.

Even though I asked Lucas about keeping my job, I decide to wait to talk to the Chief about it. I'll just take my day off today, maybe take a personal day tomorrow. I'll put off his firing me as long as possible.

An officer offers me a ride back to Aunt Pauline's but I can't face that either. I'm not going to ride in the back of a squad car ever again. I drive the cars and that's it.

I take an Uber instead.

My aunt is all aflutter when I arrive back at her house. She pounces as soon as I enter the kitchen.

"There you are. It feels like they've had you forever. Those boys. I've known them since they were in diapers, how dare they take you in like that."

"It's okay," I say, suddenly very tired.

"No, it's not. Imagine, you stabbing someone to death. Even if it is that nasty Randy."

"I know. Really, it's fine. They were just doing their jobs. Thank heavens I was here last night and not at home. Imagine being there when -. I don't want to think about it."

Aunt Pauline takes me into her arms and holds me close. I can smell the chemicals from having her hair done this morning. It's slightly nauseating, but also smells like home.

"Are you going to be okay to come to the party tonight?" she asks when she lets me go. She fills a box on the counter with plastic spoons and forks.

This darn party. I want to do anything other than be in the public, on display. I can't let her down after all she's done for me.

"I'll finally meet this mysterious Derek. It's at his house, right?"

"Yep. Out at Willow Lake. You know the place with the lake and the old mansion way in the back in the woods."

I don't know the place. Sometimes my aunt forgets I'm not a native to River Bend. She knows every inch of this town. I mostly know the meaner streets where I've patrolled the last months since I got here. I agree anyway.

She sees my confusion regardless. "Well, you can just

ride over with me. I'm heading there now to set up, then I'm coming home to change." She kisses me on the forehead like a child. "You take a nap and I'll be back in a few."

Without waiting for my response, she takes the box of plastic utensils and partyware out the door.

Alone in the kitchen, I listen to the ticking of the clock after her car drives away. The sound is soothing, rhythmic. The adrenaline I have been running on all day is long gone. I could melt into the floor.

Instead, I climb the stairs to her guest room and fall heavily onto the bed.

She'd told me to take a nap and it sounds like a good plan.

This time, when I hear the door knob rattle, I convince myself it's just a hallucination like last night.

The sound of the door swinging open is a hallucination, too.

I snuggle deeper into the pillow.

Then I hear the heavy footsteps and my eyes fly open.

The hand over my mouth is not a hallucination.

Chapter 23

GABBY

I open my computer again and then sit back in my chair as I wait for the pictures Haley is e-mailing me. A few moments later, the ding tells me the pictures arrived.

I quickly open the attachment, hoping I'll recognize whoever is in the pictures Kalissta once posted to her Facebook page, then deleted.

The man in the pictures is not familiar and my shoulders slump. I'd hoped to find a clue, something helpful. This man could be any middle-aged white guy. In all three pictures, Kalissta is taking the shot, her arm visible in the frame. In the first picture, he is looking over his shoulder at a restaurant, his face turned away. In the second, he's looking down, like he moved his head at the last minute.

In the third picture, he's kissing her cheek.

Interesting. Although I can't see his face clearly in any of the shots, I'm surprised to see him kissing her. He looks much older than she is.

"Crap on a cracker," I grumble. "This doesn't tell me anything."

I zoom in on the man's face, hoping to see something familiar, but there's nothing familiar about him. Even though I can't see his face clearly, I'm pretty sure I've never met him.

I focus on the back ground but come up with nothing there either. One is obviously taken in a restaurant. I don't go out much, but I've been to every restaurant in River Bend and this one doesn't look familiar. Of course, Kalissta is from South Bend, so it makes sense the restaurant and the man is from there, too.

Frustrated at the dead end, I close the computer and check the time. Lacey is picking me up in an hour. I think of the words scrawled on my wall. I really don't want to go home.

And I need to report it.

I pick up my phone and it rings in my hand.

Lucas's picture fills the screen and a smile fills my face.

"Hey handsome," I say. "You done with your interview?"

"We finished up a while ago. I'm fairly certain she doesn't know who killed Randy or why he's in her garage. Either she's a great liar or she's telling the truth."

I expect Kalissta is a great liar, but keep that opinion to myself.

"Have you made any headway at all? How about the UPS store angle?"

"Dustin is checking it out now. I've been working with the crime scene guys. They haven't found any fingerprints or the murder weapon. They're still combing the scene, but I don't hold out much hope."

"I'm sorry."

"I also have a call into the academy where she earned that medal. It's Saturday so I got voicemail. I'm not sure what I'm thinking to find out."

I hesitate to tell him I had Haley work that angle already, "I found out a little about that."

He laughs softly. "Dustin and I figured you would be busy on the case."

"Can't just sit around when he's targeted me, too."

Lucas grow serious. "What do you mean?"

"When I went home this morning, someone, presumably the killer, had broken in. He'd written 'come find me' on the wall in red spray paint."

"Why didn't you tell me?" he snaps. I can hear him gathering his things and picture him heading out the door of his office.

"You were busy at the other scene. I figured you'd have more luck there than at my house."

"Where are you now?" his concern is obvious.

"I'm at the shop. I need to go home to change, though. Grandma Dot and Mrs. Mott are expecting me tonight. Lacey is picking me up soon."

"Good. At least tonight you'll be with people. When you're done there, come to my house. I don't want you to be alone until we catch this guy."

"Okay," I agree, touched by his concern.

"I'll meet you at your house in ten."

"I'll be there."

I close my computer and lock the front door, then head

home.

Lucas is waiting on the street near his cruiser when I pull into my driveway. A get a familiar tingle when I look at him. I'm so glad we are back together.

"Hey," I say and give him a quick kiss.

He kisses me, but I can tell he's in cop mode and not boyfriend mode. "Let's see this message."

The door swings open when Lucas turns the knob. I half expect someone to be waiting inside, ready to jump out.

Instead, I'm met by the ugly red letters.

Lucas makes a whistling sound. "That's going to take some paint to cover." He looks around the room. "Anything else disturbed?"

I hover near the door, unsettled. "I didn't actually come in. I just got Chester and took him to Grandma's."

He nods, "Good idea." He continues searching my small house, disappearing down the hall.

I tuck my hands under my arms and step inside. The letters make my house feel dirty, violated. I want to paint over them immediately. Want them, and the writer, to disappear.

Lucas returns a short moment later. "There's no more writing and nothing obviously out of place."

I check the bathroom, the spare room and then my bedroom. "Everything looks fine. He must have done all he wanted with the paint."

"Good thing you weren't home last night," he says soberly.

"Do you think he knew I was not here? Or do you

think he came for me and settled on this?" I point to the wall.

"I think either way, I'm glad you were with me."

A shiver slides across my shoulders at the thought of how differently the night could have gone.

"Do you want to touch them?" he asks softly.

I shake my head vigorously. "I get a bad vibe just looking at them. I don't want inside his head. I don't want to know what he had planned to do if I'd been here."

"Fair enough." He pulls out his phone. "I'll get a team here to dust for fingerprints, but I honestly don't expect any. This guy has been very thorough so far."

He ducks into the kitchen and I inspect the letters closer, hoping for a clue. Maybe I should touch them. Maybe I'd see something useful. I reach a gloved hand towards the wall and an evil energy tingles through my arm.

Lucas is talking on the phone, but reaches up and pulls my hand away. "Don't."

I bow my head and wait for him to finish with his call to dispatch.

"Holy jeez, look at that!" Lacey exclaims from my open front door. I check the clock on the wall and see that it is later than I thought. "What happened?"

"I was vandalized."

"I'll say you were." Lacey steps inside my house and looks closely at the 'come find me' written on the wall. "What does this mean? Does is have to do with the serial killer on the loose?"

"How do you know about that?" Lucas asks sharply.

Lacey tosses her blond hair. "Everyone is talking about it. That and the latest murder last night. You want to make a statement?" She has the hungry look in her eyes.

"You know I won't do that," Lucas says.

"Suit yourself. I've already taped tonight's segment, anyway. You sure it's not the UPS guy that found the body?"

"Pretty sure. He had a solid alibi for all of last night. He was up with his wife and a sick kid."

"Shame," Lacey says leaning close to the words then looking up at me. "You touch them yet?"

"No. And I'm not going to."

She seems genuinely surprised. She reaches out a fingertip to the letters, then draws her hand back as if she touched something hot. "Ooh. I don't blame you."

With another toss of her hair, she's all smiles. "You ready to go?" Only then does she notice I'm dressed in baggy jeans and an old t-shirt. "You're not wearing that, are you?"

She has on a pretty flowered sundress with a jean jacket. The perfect outfit for a spring party. I have one sundress in my closet, but I'm not willing to play the who wore it best game against Lacey.

"I haven't changed yet. Just give me a minute."

I hurry to my room and throw open my closet. With a killer in town, one that has been in my house, worrying about what to wear seems silly, but I don't want to let down Grandma Dot. I pull on a pair of light blue slacks with wide legs and a linen top. I may not be as stylish as Lacey, but when I look in the mirror I look pretty good.

"Bring your swim suit," Lacey calls from the front room.

"Why? It's not really warm enough to swim in the lake."

"I hear there's a heated pool. Imagine, a pool on the lake. Mrs. Mott sure landed a good one."

"I thought he was a detective?" Lucas says as I return to the front room, a pair of sandals and my beach bag in my hand.

"That's what I was told."

Lucas's eyes widen with appreciation at my outfit, but he says, "How does a retired detective afford such an expensive house?"

I shrug and pull on a pair of fresh white gloves. "Maybe he's just renting."

"Still." Lucas rubs his stubbled face. "Maybe we should move to South Bend if detectives there can afford heated pools."

My head snaps and I meet his smoldering eyes. He's said *we*. Does that mean he wants to live with me?

"I see you two have made up," Lacey says. "Man, get a room."

"This whole place is my room," I point out.

"True. Are you ready to go? I am in the mood for a party. After all the drama we've been through, I'm ready to cut loose a little."

I shoot Lucas a questioning look. "Do you need me to stay?"

I feel like the words are staring at me and want to get away from them. I'm not as excited about going to a party as Lacey is. I'd rather work on the case. I have an ulterior motive, though. I intend to pump Mrs. Mott for info on her niece if I get the chance.

"It's better if you go. The techs will be here soon."

"Okay, then." I raise on my toes and kiss Lucas goodbye.

He leans close to my ears so Lacey can't here. "You coming to my house after the party?"

I nod against his shoulder. "Wouldn't miss it."

"I might be late. The case and all."

"I understand. I'll let myself in. I don't want to sleep here until this guy is caught. Not when he can break in." I pull away. "And I just changed the locks. Maybe I need a security system."

Lucas's face turns dark. "That might be a good idea. Whatever it takes to keep you safe."

Lacey clears her throat loudly from the open doorway.

"Sorry," I tell her. I peck Lucas on the lips and follow Lacey outside. "Techs are here." The black and yellow crime scene van has pulled up behind Lucas's cruiser. I feel eyes on my back as I walk towards Lacey's car. When I turn, I see Preston watching me out his front window. He's no doubt drawn to the police presence.

I lift my hand to wave, but the curtain falls back in place. I expect him to come outside, but he never does.

Chapter 24

GABBY

Although the ride over was slightly awkward, when I see the number of cars at Mrs. Mott's boyfriend's house, I'm glad I'm not walking into the party alone. With Lacey by my side, everyone looks at her and I can slide in mostly unnoticed. I find Grandma Dot sitting under a tent on the back lawn near the pool. She's looking out over the lake. I take the seat next to her.

"Is Mom here yet?" I ask.

"Not yet," she says and takes a sip of her drink.

"What you drinking?"

"Wine slushy."

"Ooh, I'd like one of those," Lacey says taking the seat next to mine.

"Over there," Grandma points. Lacey bobs back up.

"Want one?" she asks me.

"I'll take a Dr. Pepper if there is some."

"Knowing Pauline, there will be. She loves it almost as much as you do." When we are alone, Grandma asks me seriously. "So, how's the case? Are you all making some progress on catching this guy?"

I fiddle with the edge of the plastic tablecloth. "Not really. I talked to Haley earlier, but she didn't find much out except that Randy Benson was a real piece of work."

"The victim from this morning?"

I nod. "Looks like Kalissta had reasons to want him dead. But we know she didn't do it."

Lacey plops down beside me with a can of Dr. Pepper in one hand, a pink slushy in the other.

"You talking about the murder already?" She looks at Grandma, "Gabby won't tell me a thing." Grandma presses her lips together in an exaggerated expression. "You two are no help." Lacey scans the crowd around the tent and in the pool. "I don't see anyone I know. Hmm. Odd."

"Mostly an old lady's friends," Grandma points out.

"Where's this mysterious man who lives here?" Lacey says a with a familiar lilt to her voice.

"Pauline's boyfriend is around somewhere." Grandma emphasizes boyfriend. "He's too old for you, anyway."

Lacey tosses her hair over her shoulder. "They're never too old if they have a house like this."

Grandma shakes her head at me.

"She's harmless," I say, half-believing it. "Is Kalissta here?" I look around at the faces, not seeing her auburn hair and wide eyes.

"Now don't start anything tonight. This is supposed to be fun."

"I won't start anything. I'm just curious."

"Sure you are." Grandma doesn't believe me for a minute. "No case work tonight. A few hours of fun won't hurt you."

Mom suddenly appears over Grandma's shoulder. "Did

you see there was wine slushies?" she asks as she takes a seat at our table. "I haven't had one of those in, well decades." She makes a sound that might be a strangled laugh and bounces back out of her seat, leaving her purse on the table.

"I'll have to tell Pauline the slushies were a hit. Here she comes now." Mrs. Mott approaches our table, a pinched look on her face. "We were just talking about the slushies," Grandma tells her.

"Have you seen Kalissta?" she asks without saying hello.

"No." Grandma scans the growing crowd. "I'm sure she's here."

"When I ran home to get her, she'd left a note that she'd meet me here and that she got a ride with a friend." Mrs. Mott chews on a fingernail and looks around the tent again. "The thing is, she didn't even know about this neighborhood until I told her, let alone the address. And I haven't seen her."

"I'm sure she is fine. She and her friend probably just aren't here yet. Besides, it's hard to miss all the cars parked out front. She didn't need the actual address."

Mrs. Mott pats her hair, "Right. I know I'm being silly." She takes a deep breath. "You guys having fun?"

Mom joins us, two slushies in hand. "I'm having fun tonight if it kills me." She sucks on her straw for a long sip. "Ouch, ice cream headache."

"Take it easy, party animal," I say, glad to see Mom having fun.

"Well, if you see her, tell her I'm looking for her."

173

With a bounce of her tall hair, Mrs. Mott leaves to greet other guests.

"You want to go for a swim?" Lacey asks a while later.

I scan the pool where some kids are splashing around. The sun is glinting off the water, inviting. I haven't been swimming in a very long time and the idea of water surrounding me sounds wonderful.

"I'm definitely going," Mom says, grabbing her bag. "Coming, Gabby?"

"You guys have fun," Grandma says. One of her patrons joins her and she turns away. I follow Mom and Lacey into the large house. "Don't you think it's strange we haven't seen Mrs. Mott's boyfriend yet?"

"I have no idea what he looks like. I'm sure he's around somewhere," Mom says. "This must be the bathroom. Be right back." She ducks into the room off the hall. Lacey and I look around the living room. The room is so well decorated, I wonder if the house came with the furniture and décor already here. It looks professionally done, and I don't imagine a detective would spend money on that type of thing.

"Phew, this place is sharp," Lacey says, bending to look closely at a painting. "This is an original, not a print."

I step closer to look and she's right, the brush strokes are obvious. I don't recognize the work. "I'm not much of an art buff," I say.

"My mom is. She has several originals."

I remember Lacey's family home and all its grandeur. I'll take my tiny two-bedroom over that any day.

"How do I look?" Mom bursts out of the door and spins around. She's wearing a hot pink bikini, not too tiny, but definitely skimpier than the tankini suit I brought.

Lacey makes a whistle of appreciation. "You look great, Emily."

"You really do," I agree. And she does.

Lacey takes her turn in the bathroom to change. "Why not go in one of the guest rooms?" Mom suggests. "There's sure to be plenty of them. I can't wait to feel the water rush over my head." She nudges me down the hall toward a door that's slightly ajar.

I enter the lovely guest room and change as quickly as I can.

Lacey is changed and she and Mom are waiting impatiently. "Ready?" Mom asks.

I can't help but notice the teeny tiny lime green bikini Lacey is wearing. I suddenly feel dumpy in my dark blue tankini and boy short bottoms.

I toss my towel over my shoulder and follow them to the pool.

The water is warmer than the air as we enter the wide brick steps. A breeze brings goose bumps to my arms.

"Nice," Lacey coos, standing with the water only to her knees, posing so everyone can see her.

Mom's face is glowing as she descends the steps. "Man, how I've missed this." She suddenly dives into the water, her wake splashing me.

She surfaces and laughs like a child. Her joy makes me smile.

I step fully into the pool and, letting my skin get used

to the water. It feels amazing. I lower myself until the water touches my chin. Taking a deep breath, I sink below the surface.

The water envelopes me, washes the world away. I sit on the bottom of the pool, still and calm and listen to the quiet of the water. I stay under until my lungs begin to ache.

My arm suddenly burns.

He's watching.

I shoot to the surface and gasp for air.

Mom is floating on her back at the far end of the pool. Lacey is still on the steps, now talking to a young man.

I scan the crowd, wondering who my tattoo was talking about. I see familiar faces, men from the beauty shop or that I've seen around town. No one is watching me.

Then I see him. A glimpse of the head turning away as I see him. I don't know who the man is, but something about him feels familiar. I take a few steps across the pool to get a better look, but the man disappears into the crowd.

I suddenly don't feel like swimming.

More goose bumps cover my skin as I climb from the warm water. I find my bag and towel and wrap myself.

"Done so soon?" Lacey asks.

"Little cold for me," I lie. I really want to find the man that was watching me.

I hurry into the house to change, dripping water on the tile of the dining room as I make my way to the bedroom where I changed the first time.

The door is locked now.

I'm cold and dripping and in a hurry, so I open the next door in the hall. It's an office and looks much more like I'd imagine Mrs. Mott's Derek would have in his house.

I pull off my wet suit and shove it back into my bag. My wide pants and linen shirt stick to my damp skin and water runs off my hair. I tip upside down to wrap my towel around my head and pile it high. When I stand back up straight, I notice knives hanging on the far wall.

I bend closer to look at the display, curious. One of the knives has a speck of something dark on the blade.

I haven't put my gloves on yet and I reach out a bare hand to the speck.

The sickness slides into my mind.

Hatred, jealously, anger. She's always been mine. Slashing, cutting. Enjoyment.

I pull my hand away, my breath coming in short bursts.

This is Randy Benson's murder weapon.

"I knew you'd find it." A man's voice behind me.

Chapter 25

GABBY

I spin around and the man that was watching me swim stands in the doorway. He seems vaguely familiar. Then I realize where I've seen him before. Kalissta's deleted pictures.

"You're Derek, aren't you?"

He smiles slyly. "That isn't a hard deduction to make. Not like the one with that knife. I left it on display just in case you decided to snoop around. I knew you would."

I lift my chin, fight the urge to run. It would be hopeless anyway, he's much taller than me and despite his age, he's much broader and muscled than I ever will be. "You stabbed Randy Benson to death with this knife?" I ask, stalling.

"You already know I did," he says enigmatically.

"But why?"

"Oh, the eternal question. Haven't you figured it out yet?"

"Because he was bothering Kalissta. But what does it have to do with you? Because she's Mrs. Mott's niece?"

He shakes his head slowly. "Oh, Gabby, you can do better than that." He leans against the door jamb as if he has all the time in the world. "Try again."

179

"You're obsessed with her. You want her."

He snaps upright. "She's mine. She has been since the first day she walked into my class at the academy. It didn't take long until I'd proven to her we were meant to be."

"You two had an affair?"

"You make it sound dirty. You could never understand what we had. In the end, she didn't understand either and broke it off with me."

"That was a long time ago."

"Time doesn't matter when you're talking about destiny." His brown eyes have turned nearly black. The same eyes I saw behind the mask in Shelly Parker's murder.

"Why all the murders? What did all those innocent people have to do with you?"

"I did your excuse of a town a favor. I was just cleaning up what your boyfriend and brother never could. Plus, and more importantly, I was testing Kalissta the way I used to at the academy. That's the whole reason I came to River Bend. It was only a matter of time until she realized it was me doing all that for her. Then she'd realize what a pair we make. When you stepped in I had to put my game in fast forward."

"Where's Kalissta now? Mrs. Mott hasn't seen her." I look over his shoulder, wondering if anyone else is in the house, if someone will come to distract him long enough that I can run.

"She's here. You just didn't look in the right place."

Before I can wonder at his cryptic words, he pounces. I don't have time to react before his arm is against my throat in a choke hold. I pull on his arm, but he uses the other hand to force a rag against my face.

I try not to breathe. The chemical on the rag burns my eyes and I squeeze them shut. I kick back as hard as I can, but my feet are still bare from swimming and glance off his legs.

"Keep fighting. It makes this more fun," he hisses in my ear. My lungs ache and I need air. Against my will, my mouth opens and I suck in the horrible chemicals.

My vision dims and the room spins.

"That's a good girl," he croons. "Nighty, night."

The last things I hear are my mom calling "Gabby, you in here?" and the door locking as Mrs. Mott's wonderful new boyfriend, Derek, leaves me unconscious on the office floor.

Chapter 26

GRANDMA DOT

"She wasn't in the house," Emily says as she takes her seat next to me at the table under the green and white striped tent.

"I saw her go in a while ago." A patron I haven't seen in a few months approaches our table. I notice her roots are done, not grown out. She's been going to another stylist.

I plaster on a smile like it doesn't bother me and prepare to make polite talk.

Emily fidgets in her seat, her wine slushy melting in its cup.

When the ex-patron finally leaves, I turn my attention to my daughter. "Stop worrying. Gabriella's around her somewhere. Probably just talking to a friend where we can't see her."

I don't believe the words as they leave my mouth. Gabriella doesn't have many friends, at least not ones that are at this party. I check the pool and see Lacey still standing on the steps in her lime green bikini, making sure everyone sees her. "Have you asked Lacey where she might be?"

"Does it look like Lacey is paying attention to anything other than the young men?"

"Good point." I pat Emily's hand, "I'm sure she's around somewhere."

Apprehension bubbles in my belly. It's not like Gabriella to leave and not say good-bye. Besides, she rode here with Lacey so she doesn't have her car.

"I'm going to check the house again. Maybe I missed her."

Pauline approaches our table and Emily sits back down. "You guys having fun?"

I nod, but my best friend doesn't believe me.

"Then why do you both look so worried?"

"I can't find Gabby," Emily says.

Pauline looks over her shoulder and scans the crowd. Her face is pinched when she turns back to us. "I still haven't seen Kalissta, either. You don't think they are together. I can't imagine the sparks that would fly from that encounter."

From everything I heard about last night's incident, I don't imagine Gabriella would be palling around with Pauline's niece.

Emily says, "Can you imagine?"

"This is getting ridiculous, where did those two girls get off to?" I stand from the table and go to Lacey. She looks surprised and slightly annoyed when I approach. The man she was talking to backs away a few feet. "Lacey, have you seen Gabriella?"

Lacey looks into the pool, "I thought she was

swimming."

"She got out quite a while ago. We can't find her."

Lacey seems more concerned with the young man waiting for me to leave than with looking for Gabriella. "I'm sure she's around someplace."

"If you see her, let her know Emily and I are looking for her."

Lacey pushes her long hair over her shoulder. I notice goose-bumps on her arm and think she must be freezing. It's a lovely April day and unseasonably warm, but not really warm enough to be posing in a bikini. "Will do." She turns her attention back to the man.

Emily is watching me from our table and I raise my hands in an "I don't know" gesture. I return to the table and sit down heavily, worry pulling at me.

"I'm checking the house," Emily says. I follow her inside the large, well-appointed home. Derek is in the kitchen taking ice from the freezer and putting it in a large tub. He smiles brightly as we enter.

"Dot, I'm sorry I haven't come to say hi yet. So many people to greet, you know how it is."

"Derek, this is my daughter Emily. We're looking for Gabby. Have you seen her?"

His face is blank, "I don't think so. Of course, I haven't had the pleasure of meeting her officially yet."

"Do you mind if we look around a little?" Emily asks.

"Of course not. Look away, but I've been in the kitchen here for a while now and I haven't seen her."

Emily doesn't even wait for him to finish his sentence when she marches down the hall calling Gabriella's name.

The bathroom is empty, the guest room is empty. The office and the master bedroom are both locked to keep prying eyes out.

We return to the kitchen and Derek. "Sorry, I told you I didn't see her come in. If she turns up, I'll send her your way. I'm sure she's around."

"Have you seen Kalissta?" I ask.

Derek's face shifts a fraction then resumes the smooth look. "I haven't yet met her either. I don't think she came to the party."

"She told Pauline she'd meet her here but she hasn't turned up," Emily says.

"Girls will be girls. Maybe they're together."

"You obviously don't know either of them," I say.

"Well, Pauline needs this ice. I'd better get back to the party," Derek says and goes out through the sliding patio door to the pool area. I watch him go to Pauline and hand her the tub of ice.

The house is so quiet, I can hear the fridge motor kick on. "Well, I don't know where else to look."

Emily is chewing at her fingernail in agitation. "Maybe she got a call about a case and left."

"She wouldn't have left without telling one of us."

"You don't think we are over-reacting. I mean it's only been half an hour."

"When Gabriella's concerned, there's no such thing as over-reacting." I fish my cell phone out of my pocket and dial Dustin.

"Grandma, everything okay?" he asks with a mixture of confusion and concern.

186

"I don't know," I say honestly. "I think Gabriella is missing."

He sighs heavily. "Where are you?"

"We're at Pauline Mott's party in Willow Lake. Kalissta Hawthorne is missing, too."

"We'll be right there."

Chapter 27

LUCAS

I look up from the surveillance tape from the UPS store at Dustin's concerned, "We'll be right there."

"What's wrong?"

He looks around the room instead of at me, fidgets with his shirt pocket. "That was Grandma Dot, she thinks Gabby is missing."

I feel the blood drain from my face. "I thought they were at a party."

"They are. She can't find Gabby."

I glance back at the tape, reach toward the computer to turn it off. The part we needed to see, the time when the suspect shipped the medal to Kalissta appears before I push the keys. A man dressed in sunglasses and a hat is handing a box to the clerk.

I lean closer to the screen. "Does he look familiar?" I ask Dustin.

He looks but shakes his head. "Hard to tell. He obviously knew he'd be taped and took precautions."

I'm eager to leave and look for Gabby but if she's truly missing, the man on this tape likely has something to do with it. The man turns his head, and his salt and pepper sideburn is in full view. Something about his profile seems familiar.

"Wait a minute." I take out my phone and open the file Gabby sent me earlier of the pictures Kalissta deleted. One of them shows the man's sideburns. I hold the phone up to the computer screen and compare the pictures.

"Does this look like the same man?"

Dustin looks at both pictures and agrees with me. "It really does. Where'd you get those?"

"Gabby got them from Haley who found them when she was checking out Kalissta. They were deleted from her Facebook account."

Dustin takes my phone and looks closer. "I think I know this guy."

"Really?" I shut the computer lid and grab the cruiser keys.

"I met him a while back at Grandma Dot's. It looks like Mrs. Mott's new boyfriend, Derek. It's hard to tell, but it looks like him."

I squeeze the keys hard in my hand. "Isn't that where this party is?"

"Yes." Dustin follows me from the office. "Grandma said she thinks Kalissta is missing, too. He must have them both."

"This can't be good." I walk as quickly as I can to the parking garage and climb into the cruiser. "Call this in. If we are right we are going to need all the help we can get."

As soon as I get on the road, I flip on the lights and sirens and punch the gas. "We're coming, Gabby."

As we enter the neighborhood, I turn off the sirens, but hurry to Derek's house. It's easy to find the house, the large green and white tent and all the cars parked on the streets gives it away. The driveway has been blocked off by two small caution cones. One of them is lying on its side. I ignore the cones and park in front of the garage.

We jump out of the car and Grandma and Emily come around the side of the house to greet us.

"We still haven't found her," Emily says. "Now Derek is missing, too."

"If we're right, Derek has them."

Mrs. Mott joins us in time to hear Dustin say that. Her hand flies to her hair, "That can't be. Not my Derek."

I put my hand on her shoulder, "We don't know anything for sure, yet. Mrs. Mott did Derek ever mention that he knew Kalissta?"

She shakes her head, "Of course not. They are both cops from South Bend, but Derek was retired by the time Kalissta started working there. I don't see how they ever met. Oh my, why?"

"Kalissta had pictures of him and her together on her Facebook page a long time ago. She deleted them, but we found them. It looks like they more than knew each other. Didn't Kalissta tell you when she found out you were dating him?"

"They never met and I don't know if she knew his last name. Oh no, this is all my fault."

"No it isn't, Pauline," Grandma Dot says gently. "Sounds like this is all Derek's doing. None of that matters now. We have to find Gabriella."

Emily gasps, "Does that mean Derek killed that young man at Kalissta's house? Wait, and all the other victims?"

191

her voice raises towards hysteria. "And he has Gabby."

Dustin takes his mom's shoulder in his hand. "Now stay calm, Mom. Gabby can handle herself, I'm sure she is fine. But we need to find her." He looks to Mrs. Mott. "Derek isn't here? Where would he go?"

Lacey appears around the side of the house in time to hear the question. "What's going on? Did you guys have a break in the case?"

"Sort of," I say. "Gabby and Kalissta have been taken and it looks like Derek took them."

"He said he was running to the store," Lacey says. "I was out front here having a smoke and I saw the car pull out of the garage. He rolled his window down and said he was running for more chips and would be right back."

"How long ago was that?"

"Maybe ten minutes."

"Was Gabby with him?" I ask.

"Not that I saw."

I look at Dustin. "He must have had her in the trunk."

Emily gasps again. "Go get her."

I direct my attention to Mrs. Mott. "Do you know where he might have taken her, and Kalissta," I add. "Anywhere he likes to go, somewhere secluded."

She shakes her head, her hair bouncing. "No. I mean, he's new to town. Where would he take them? I can't believe this."

"Getting upset won't help. For now, let's talk to everyone and see if someone saw something. Go tell your guests that no one leaves until we tell them they can." She hurries out back to spread the news.

I look to Grandma, "Where's the last place you saw Gabby?"

"I saw her go in the house to change out of her swimsuit," Emily volunteers. "As far as I saw, she never came back out."

"Let's start inside."

Dustin leads the way through the front door. "Where would she have changed?" I ask Emily.

"She changed first in the guest room, but we already checked there. The other doors are locked."

I check out the guest room and it is empty. The next door is closed and I turn the knob.

"That room was locked," Grandma says.

The knob turns and the door opens. "Not locked now," I say.

Inside on the floor is Gabby's straw beach bag, her towel is dropped next to it. Her phone is under the desk.

"It was locked, I promise," Grandma says.

"He probably had her in here," Dustin says, crouching next to Gabby's things.

"We were right outside the door," Emily says. "So close, my baby."

"Stay calm. We will find her."

Lacey has been quietly following us, but speaks up now. "Grandma, can I talk to you for a minute."

They duck into the hall and I look around the room. A display of knives is on the wall above the desk. It reminds me of the displays filling Kalissta's house. I lean closer and a small spot of blood on one of the blades catches my eye.

"Dustin, look. I think this might be the murder weapon that killed Randy Benson."

Dustin scrutinizes the knife, "That does look like blood. If Gabby was in here, maybe she saw it, too."

"It's worth a try," Grandma says to Lacey out in the hall.

I step out, a question on my face. "Lacey has an idea," Grandma says, pushing past me into the office.

She picks up the towel and bag, holds it close to her chest. "You know I have a bit of Gabby's gift, well so does Lacey."

I'm surprised at this, Lacey never let on one bit about it. "Of course, we have only a fraction of what Gabby has, but maybe we can reach her somehow."

I'm willing to try anything.

Lacey stands close to Grandma, holds her hand and closes her eyes. "What does Gabby always say? Lord, let me see what needs to be seen?"

We all repeat the prayer, our heads bowed.

Lacey takes in a sudden breath, moans a little. A moment later, she drops Grandma's hand and steps back.

"Did you see her?"

Lacey swallows hard, "It was dim, but I saw a window and a fireplace with an ornate mantle. A fancy room, but it's covered in dust and there's only a few pieces of furniture."

Mrs. Mott is suddenly at the door to the office, "That sounds like the abandoned mansion at the far end of the lake."

194

Chapter 28

GABBY

His voice swims into my head. "Don't be scared. I did this all for you. You were meant to be mine."

Her voice, tiny and afraid, answers. "You did this all for me?"

"For you, my dearest, Kalissta. We could be a team."

My head is foggy, the words sound far away. I try to open my eyes, but can only manage slits. Next to me is Kalissta tied to a chair, Derek is kneeling before her, pleading. He wears the white plastic mask I saw in my visions. The mask startles me. Why wear it now? We already know his identity.

I try to lift my hand, but something that feels like a zip tie, cuts into my wrist. Panic surges as I try to move. My hands and feet are bound to a chair, like Kalissta's.

"I want that," she's saying. "Please untie me and I'm yours."

I blink and the two come into better focus. A knife appears in his hand and hovers over Kalissta's zip ties. "You really mean it, truly?" He sounds so lovesick it increases my nausea. I gag against the rag shoved in my mouth.

He turns his masked face to me, "She's awake." With a

flash of the blade, he cuts Kalissta's ties on her wrists. "Now the fun can start." He bends and cuts her ankles free.

She rushes into his outstretched arms. "I've missed you," she says against his chest.

"I didn't know Aunt Pauline's Derek was you or I would have come to you sooner."

He holds her face in his palms, gently strokes her cheek. "All part of the plan, my dear."

His focus shifts to me. Now that he's not looking at her Kalissta seems terrified, her eyes pleading with me. I wonder if she's really giving into the madman's desires or if she's faking it.

"Now, Gabby let's get started." He stands and pulls the rag from my mouth.

"Why the mask. I already know who you are?" I ask, my voice groggy, my tongue dry.

"I feel more like my true self in this." He touches the edge of it with a tender finger.

"Where are we?" I ask.

"The abandoned mansion across the lake from my house. I love coming here. Did you know a man killed his entire family in the rooms upstairs?"

"It is a legend in River Bend. Of course I know."

"So feisty. You're kind of a legend here, too."

Kalissta stands behind his shoulder and watches me. I want her to hit him, to knock the knife from his hand, something to save us. She leans into his shoulder.

"Derek, why is she here?"

"It's a mixture of curiosity and the need for your help,"

he says to me.

"Why would I help you?" I practically spit.

"Because, deep down, we want the same thing, to stop crime."

"You're a crime fighter then?"

"Among other things. I came into this town because Kalissta was here, but I decided to help the police while I was at it. Rid the town of the lowlifes that are bringing it down."

"Andy Tippins and Shelly Parker were struggling, but I wouldn't call them lowlifes."

"I would. Doesn't matter now. This town is better without them and all the others."

"I don't think their families would agree."

"I don't care about their families," he shouts, making both Kalissta and me jump. "What I care about is my mission." He leans so close I can see the red veins in his eyes. "They needed to go. And before you ask, Randy didn't deserve to live, either. Not after what he did to my sweet Kalissta." He lifts himself away and runs a hand over Kalissta's hair. The gesture would seem sweet in another place.

"I thank you for that," she says.

"I don't want to help you."

"You will want to do this. It is right up your alley."

At the far end of the room is a dining table covered in what looks like police files. He shuffles through the files, then pulls one out.

"This here," he says waving the file in the air. "It's a good place to start. This is a cold case that South Bend

PD has been working on for more than fifteen years. I want you to tell me what you see."

My stomach sinks as I realize why he brought me here. He wants to test me, to use me.

I wriggle against my ties, but only get pain in my wrists and ankles. "I won't do it."

"You will." He lifts the fingers of my bare left hand and places the file between my hand and the arm of the chair. "Now do your magic and give me a clue to this case."

I brace myself for a rush of unwanted vision, but nothing comes.

"I'm getting nothing."

"Try harder," he shouts. Kalissta flinches, but smiles a tight smile.

I close my eyes and focus on the folder. "Seriously, I'm getting nothing."

He suddenly laughs so loud it echoes through the room. "Nicely done." He opens the folder and there is nothing inside. "I had to make sure you weren't going to try to trick me."

"So you tricked me?"

"Just a test. I like tests. I really enjoyed my short time at the police academy as a visiting instructor. I came up with all kinds of tests for the recruits." He looks to Kalissta. "Plus, I met my true love." He returns to the table and riffles through the files again. "Ahh, this is a good one."

He shoves the folder under my bare hand. This time a vision pumps through me.

A familiar face. Disbelief. Cold water and hard metal underneath. Unbearable pain in my throat.

I cough and gag and tip the chair away from the folder.

"So, your gift is real. What did you see?"

"A young woman was strangled. She knew her killer and couldn't believe what he was doing. She was left in a drainage culvert, wasn't she?"

He claps his hands against the file in applause. "Well done. That was awesome. Of course, we already knew all that. Well, except the part about her knowing her killer. You got all that just from touching the file?"

I look away from his masked face, "I did."

"Can you believe this?" he asks Kalissta.

"She is something. Do another."

"Not yet." He kneels before me again. "Will you join us? The three of us could be quiet a team. Think of all the cases we could clear."

"So you could kill the suspects?"

He shrugs, "All part of the mission. They will get what they deserved."

"It's not up to you to kill them. Only God can decide when someone should die."

He laughs again, "Silly girl. I can play God."

I feel dirty being so close to such madness.

Behind his back, Kalissta is looking around the room, her eyes focus on something behind me. She darts her gaze to me, then back to whatever is behind me.

"You sure you won't join us?" he coos, running a hand down my leg, his touch hot through the thin fabric of my pants. I try to kick him, but the plastic tie cuts into my ankle.

He looks over his shoulder, "She always this much trouble?" he asks Kalissta.

"She's not worth it." Kalissta walks behind me. I struggle to keep my eyes on her.

That's when I see it.

The entire wall is covered in fireworks.

"What's that?" I ask, panic flooding my brain. I've never liked fireworks. Dustin once burned himself badly when we were kids and I've had a healthy respect for their power ever since.

"This," Derek says with a flourish, is for you if you don't agree to join me."

He stands and turns my chair so I'm facing the wall of colorful, glittering danger.

It's an impressive display and it makes my blood run cold.

"W-what are you going to do?"

"Join me. Join us," he demands.

I look him in the eye. "Never."

"Then we have nothing left to discuss." He takes Kalissta by the hand. I don't know if I see her flinch or if that's wishful thinking.

"Kalissta, you can't let him do this," I beg as he takes a lighter from his pocket.

She looks to Derek then back to me, her eyes pleading. "I'm sorry, Gabby," she says.

Derek suddenly turns towards the front door. "I think I hear your boyfriend out there."

"Derek, we know you're in there. Come out and no one

gets hurt," Lucas shouts from the front lawn.

"Oh, I'm coming out, but you're not." He takes Kalissta by the hand and together they light the fuse that ties the fireworks together. It sizzles and sputters. For a moment, I think it's going to burn out but it stays lit.

"Last chance to join us. You still have time to run if you just agree."

I look from the burning fuse to his masked face.

"Derek, come out now," Lucas shouts.

"I'll take my chances."

"It was nice meeting you." He pulls Kalissta with him towards the back of the house.

"Gabby, change your mind," she shouts.

The fuse reaches the first of the fireworks and they explode in a fountain of sparks. "Lucas, get in here!" I scream, pushing with my feet to slide my chair across the wood floor. "He's gone and the house is on fire. Get in here."

I push hard and slide backwards until the chair catches on the edge of a rug and tips over. I land hard on my back, the chair pressing into me. A firework whizzes across the room and hits the drapes. From the corner of my eye, I see them catch fire.

I scream for help as more fireworks catch and explode, shooting fire around the room.

Over the bangs and whistles, I hear the front door being pounded as Lucas tries to break it down. The heavy wood won't budge.

"The window!" I shout against the smoke.

Glass shatters into the room as Lucas barrels through

the wide front windows. "Gabby what is that?" he shouts and rushes to my side, ducking the firebombs.

"Fireworks and they're catching the house on fire." The burning drapes have fallen from the window and landed on the floor in a pile of flame, catching the floor on fire. Lucas uses his pocket knife and cuts my ties.

"Where's Derek and Kalissta?" he shouts as my first hand comes free.

"He took her to the back of the house."

"Dustin, he's headed to the back of the house."

Dustin looks in through the front window, indecision on his face. "Go for him. We got this," I shout.

Both hands are now free and Lucas is working on my ankle. Behind him, the wall is going wild, sparks fly in every direction in a shower of light. The ceiling is now on fire and the air is thick with smoke.

I cough and sputter as he cuts the last tie. "We have to get out of here," he shouts over the din of the flames and explosions.

The floor between us and the front door is full of flames, the heat scorching my face. Now that I'm free, I get on my hands and knees and crawl for the front window where Lucas came in.

Glass crunches under my knees, but I ignore the pain. I raise myself over the window sill and belly crawl out into the fresh air. As I land in the bushes, I turn to make sure Lucas is behind me.

He's standing in the window, ready to climb out when he suddenly slumps forward, half in and half out the window.

I jump up screaming his name. His hair is on fire and blood is pouring from his scalp. A round, burning lump is in the bushes. He's been hit in the head by a firework mortar.

I say his name over and over and pat out the flames in his hair. He's limp and not responding. Smoke billows out the window and flames fill the house.

Grabbing his arm, I pull with all my strength. He moves a few inches out the window. I take a breath, then pull again. His weight slides out the window, tumbling me into the bushes. His unconscious body lands on top of me, pinning me to the ground between two overgrown bushes.

I struggle to breathe, struggle to move. I wriggle and squirm until I get out from under him. An explosion inside makes me duck. Several balls of sparkles shoot out the window, dropping sparks on us.

I grab both his wrists and pull him out of the bushes. I drag him heavily away from the burning house. My hands grow slick with sweat and I lose my grip. I reposition and pull again. Little by little, I cross the yard, fireworks shooting at us the whole time.

Once I reach a tree that gives us some cover, I can inspect his injuries.

His head is split open and his hair is singed, but he's still breathing. I check the pulse in his neck and feel his heart racing.

"Lucas, Lucas, wake up." I gently smack the unburned side of his face. He moans a little but remains unconscious. Not knowing what else to do, I cradle his head in my lap and use the hem of my shirt to stop the bleeding. The white linen is soon turned bright red.

From the corner of my eye, the corner of my consciousness, I see Derek's car burst down the driveway and Dustin chasing after it.

I don't care about Derek. I only have room for Lucas.

I take the radio from his shoulder, click the button and say, "Officer down," to whoever is listening.

Chapter 29

KALISSTA

As much as I didn't like Gabby last night, I never expected this for her. As Derek pulls me through the house, I want to go back to help her.

But I have to help myself. Derek believes I'm on his side, but I'm just faking it until I can escape.

"Sorry, Gabby," I say to myself as we run into the garage.

His car is parked inside.

"You sure about this?" he asks as he opens the passenger door for me. He always opened doors for me when we were dating. It was part of why I liked him so much. It feels out of place here.

"I'm sure," I lie.

He falls for it and lets me into the car.

I take my seat, my mind racing for a way out of this as he makes his way around the car. He stops near the garage door and throws it open. He then hurries into the car, starts it and peels out in reverse.

As we barrel down the driveway, I see Detective McAllister running after us across the yard. Good, that means Lucas is here and Gabby is going to be saved.

Now I just have to save myself.

The lake glitters at the far end of the yard and it gives me an idea.

"Almost there," Derek says and pulls off his mask. He throws it in the backseat, then grins at me. "Just you and me."

A cruiser is suddenly in front of us and I see Officer Patterson's surprised face through the windshield.

Derek shouts in surprise.

It's the distraction I needed.

I grab the wheel and pull hard, the car careening towards the water. Patterson follows as we bump across the yard. Derek shouts, "What are you doing?" and tries to wrestle the steering wheel away from me.

I don't let go, direct us to the lake.

He slams on the brakes, but it's too late. The car lurches down the bank and into the water.

The cold lake seeps into the car as we float a moment then begin to sink. He takes a gun from his waistband.

"Why did you do that?" he says low and menacing.

"I-I-." I have no explanation that will fix the situation. "I got scared."

"You've ruined everything." He looks down at the rapidly rising water. Outside the car, the water is to the windows. "We're sinking. Open your door." I know it won't open it will only open when the car is full of water and the pressure is equalized. I fake it and try anyway.

I turn on the best performance of my life, "Derek, I'm sorry. I just got scared when I saw that cop coming after us. Please don't let me die like this."

His expression wavers, wanting to believe me. I press

on.

"I love you. I'm yours. Please, put the gun down."

He looks at the gun like he forgot it was in his hand. The water has reached our waists. I fight the panic searing in my blood.

Just wait until you can open the doors. Just play it cool.

My life depends on what he does next.

He puts the gun on the dash.

I grab it and point it at his head.

"What?" he exclaims.

"You killed all those people."

"I did it for you."

The water has nearly covered the car, only a fraction of an inch of sky is visible on the windows. Outside the car the water is growing darker, blocking out the sun.

Inside the car the moment is tense.

"For me? You know that is crazy, right?"

In the fading light, shivering in the rising water, he doesn't look like the brilliant visiting marksmanship instructor I remember, the alluring man I fell in love with.

He just looks old.

His eyes dart around the car at the rising water. He tries to open the door, a useless endeavor. "We have to get out of here. We're going to drown."

Old and panicked. Nothing like the man I thought he was.

"You tricked my aunt, made her believe in you. She liked you a lot."

"That was all for you," he tries to persuade me. "So I

207

could be close to you."

The water is up to our chins now and I'm holding the gun above the water line.

"You hurt her."

He suddenly lunges for the gun and I pull the trigger.

The shot makes my ears ring. As if in slow motion, his head snaps back and I see a hole formed in his neck. The window behind him shatters and water pours in, forcing the last few inches of air out of the car.

I have to escape or die trying.

I take a deep breath from the last of the air, my mouth so close to the top of the car I can feel the fabric touch my lips.

I drop the gun and climb over his body, pushing against the rush of water. I force my way out of the shattered window and kick for the surface.

I don't raise towards the air, Derek has grabbed my ankle. I pull at his fingers, kick at his hand with my other foot.

A shadow slides through the water and Officer Patterson is hitting Derek in the face.

He lets go of my ankle and I shoot upwards, my lungs burning.

I burst to the surface and gasp, taking in the sweetness of the air.

Patterson surfaces next to me. "You okay?"

I nod and say a shivery, "I think so."

"I have to save him." He takes a deep breath and goes back under.

I swim towards the shore where McAllister is waiting

for me. He grabs my hand and helps me out of the water.

Patterson surfaces again, but doesn't have Derek with him.

"I can't find him."

He ducks under again and returns without him. "I don't think he's in the car," he says confused.

I scan the lake, expecting to see Derek somewhere. Besides the activity where Patterson is, the lake is calm.

Patterson surfaces again, breathlessly he says. "He's gone."

Chapter 30

GABBY

It's been six days since Lucas was knocked unconscious. It's been six days that he's been in a coma. It's been six days since I've left his side except for quick trips home to shower every now and then.

Today, Lucas's dad, Gregor, sits with me. Every day, someone comes. Every day I wish they would leave.

Gregor sits forward suddenly, rubs his face with his hands. "He's in there, right?" he asks me looking at his son's still body.

The question I've asked God so many times. God hasn't answered me, but I have to believe. "He's there. I know he is."

The doctors are not as sure as I am. They can't give us answers. They can only tell me time will show us.

I don't want to wait.

"Can't you do your thing and find out?" Gregor asks. "I hear you did it before with that girl in a coma."

"I did that, but this is different. I've never been able to read Lucas like I can strangers."

Gregor rubs his face again. "I suppose that makes

sense." He stands suddenly. "I need some air. I'll be back tomorrow."

I sit alone and listen to the monitor that plays me Lucas's heartbeat. The rhythmic sound lulls.

"Gabby?" Dustin whispers, startling me. I must have dozed off.

I sit up, check Lucas's vitals and then say hi.

"Any change?"

"No. Nothing."

Dustin rubs his hands together in agitation. "This sucks," he finally says, taking the seat Gregor just left. This isn't the first time he's been to visit. Each time he comes, he looks a little paler, a little more drawn.

"How's Alexis?" I ask, eager to talk about anything other than the hell I'm in.

His face brightens. "She's doing well. We've had several talks about what went wrong. She told me you knew."

"I only knew for a while. It wasn't my place to tell you," I defend myself.

"I know that. It's okay. I should have paid more attention, been there for her."

"I'm just glad it's all out in the open now. She needs all of us to recover."

He sits forward. "How are you holding up? I mean, really?" Ever since the accident, Dustin has been the supportive brother he never was in the past. Lucas's coma has affected him deeply.

"I'm hanging in there." I look at Lucas's unshaven face, his mussed hair. He looks like he's sleeping, but he won't wake up.

"You have to take care of yourself. Lucas wouldn't forgive us if we let you waste away while he's gone."

"I'm not wasting away. Grandma comes by every day and brings me food." Dustin looks out the window a moment, lost in thought. "Something's up. What is it?" I ask.

"I'm not sure this is the right time to talk about it."

"Did they find Derek? Grandma said they searched the lake for his body."

"No. They didn't find him, but that's not what I want to talk about."

"Then spill it."

"Chief Simmons came to me with a proposition today."

"What was that?"

"He wants me to ask you how you'd feel about hiring on as a consultant for us. It's an actual job."

I'm shocked. It's one thing for Dustin to pretend I am one, another if I actually worked for them.

"How do you feel about that?" I hedge.

"I think it would help keep you out of trouble if you actually were on our team instead of chasing leads on your own."

"Hey, I was just at a party when Derek took me. It's not my fault," I defend myself.

"I know." His eyes flicker over Lucas and away again. "So, what do you say? Will you at least think about it?"

"I don't have to think about it. I'm in."

"Really? Because we have all these cases Derek might

or might not have committed. It would really help if you could at least tell us which ones were murders and which were suicides or accidents. We have to go through all the cases since Derek first arrived in River Bend."

"I can do that. But can it wait?"

His gaze flickers over Lucas again and then back out the window. "Of course."

"How's Kalissta?" I ask, changing the subject.

"She's back to work. I don't really talk to her, but she seems okay."

"That's good." I pat Lucas's hand and the silence in the room grows, only the sound of the monitor beeping.

"Well, then." Dustin stands and heads for the door. He looks back, focuses on Lucas for the first time. "Get better, buddy. We all need you." His voice cracks and he hurries from the room.

I sit alone with the monitor. "Did you hear that?" I say out loud to Lucas. "A consultant. An actual job working with you. I'm no longer the freak."

The monitor beeps faster, and I take it as a sign that he hears me.

I think of what Gregor asked me. If I could reach him, know he's still there somehow.

Lucas's hand is cool through my glove. I have never been able to read anything when I touch him in the past, today I will try.

"I'm going to do something," I tell his inert body as I take off my gloves. "I need you to talk to me. Please."

I put my left hand directly over his chest and place my right over my cross tattoo. I bow my head and pray like

I've never prayed before.

"God, I need all your power now. Please let me see."

I close my eyes and open myself to Lucas.

A flicker of emotion skitters through my head.

Love.

"Please. Please show me," I beg.

Two words. The best two words I've ever heard.

I'm here.

Tears sting my eyes as I pull my hand off his chest.

He's here. He's fighting.

I lower my wet face to his chest. I listen to him breathe, listen to his heart beating under my cheek.

"Come back to me," I beg for the hundredth time.

He breathes on, steady and shallow.

The monitor beeps faster, then suddenly slows. I sit back, listening. Something is wrong.

"Lucas?" I say as his always steady heart begins to beat erratically.

His face grows pale beneath his week's worth of stubble. "Lucas! Wake up."

Panic like I've never felt before blooms wild in my chest. I run to the door, "Nurse, nurse. Something's wrong," I shout down the hall.

A nurse hurries to the room. She takes one look at the monitor and rushes to his bedside.

The little lines on the monitor are jumping around. Nothing like the steady readout they've been. Another nurse joins us and they begin to work on him.

My ears pound with fear and everything slows down. Vaguely, I hear the overhead speaker call a code. It takes a moment until I realize the code is for Lucas.

People crowd the room and I'm pushed aside.

From the corner of the room, I watch them try to revive the man I love. I listen to his heartbeat slow and jump. Then the horrible sound of a flatline.

They pull out the crash paddles and shock his heart. I watch as his limp body bounces from the shock, my vision blurred from tears.

"No, no, no," I say over and over. "Lucas, you fight!" I scream. "You come back to me!"

I watch in horror as they shock him again, expect him to wake up, expect him to move or give me some sign he will be okay.

I don't get the sign.

I drop to my knees and pray. I can't make words, all I can say, is, "Please, please, please."

Through my terror, I feel my tattoo tingle.

I listen, rapt with hope.

Not yet.

I scream in victory. The medical staff grows quiet and the monitor seems so loud.

The steady beat of his heart is back.

I push them aside and fall onto his chest, crying and panting. I feel someone rubbing my hair and lift my head.

"I'm here," Lucas says. "I'm here."

His blue eyes bore into mine.

He's alive and awake.

Even with the bandage, Lucas looks handsome in his button up shirt and khaki shorts that he's worn to

Grandma Dot's family dinner.

"Looking good," Grandma says as we enter the kitchen that smells like fried chicken.

"He does look good, doesn't he?" I say, giving her a heartfelt hug. I pull away and see the tray of Rice Krispy treats. "Mind if I have dessert first?"

Grandma hands me one, "I made them for you. I know they are your favorite."

Jet jumps on my leg, wanting a nibble. I pull off a small part of the treat and hand it to him. He scarfs it down and dances for more.

Chester watches from across the kitchen. I take my cat in my arms. "Thank you for watching Chester these last weeks," I say.

"My pleasure. He and Jet get along well. Besides, you've had your hands full."

"That's an understatement," Lucas says. "But the doctors have cleared me. At least enough to be home now."

"Look at you, up and around," Dustin says coming into the kitchen from the living room. He clasps Lucas on the shoulder. "So glad to see you here." The men share a meaningful glance that I don't understand.

"Dinner will be a while, let's sit in the living room," Grandma says. I've never known her to leave the kitchen while making Sunday dinner, but I follow her into the other room.

Lucas hangs behind.

Alexis is sitting on the couch next to Mom, Walker is playing with blocks on the floor in front of her. Dustin sits down and puts his arm around her shoulders. I'm glad to see them getting along so well.

I sit in one of the arm chairs, wondering where Lucas has disappeared to.

Everyone is giving me sly looks. "What?" I finally ask.

Lucas is suddenly in front of me, taking my hand and having me stand.

"How's the Rice Krispy treats?" he asks.

"Good as always," I say, confused.

"Eat up," he smiles.

I take another bite and hit something hard.

"What's this?" I ask, not wanting to dare dream.

He takes the treat, fishes out the ring and drops to his knee. I burst into happy tears.

"Gabby, I've known you since we were kids and you played with my sister. I think I loved you then and I've never stopped." He peels my glove off my hand. I can barely breathe. I never thought I'd have this life. Never thought I'd find love like I have with him.

I'm nodding before he can utter the words, "Will you marry me?"

I squeal a yes and he slides the precious silver ring onto my finger. "Yes, yes, a thousand times, yes."

Crap on a cracker, I'm getting married.

The End

Want more books by Dawn Merriman? Check them all out at http://viewauthor.at/DawnMerriman on Amazon.

Follow Dawn Merriman by joining her fan club on Facebook at https://www.facebook.com/groups/dawnmerrimannovelist fanclub

Sign up for her newsletter at www.DawnMerriman.com

If you loved this book please leave a review on Amazon.

Note from Dawn Merriman,

Crap on a cracker, Gabby has come a long way. From sitting alone at the superstore at the beginning of book one to getting married and surrounded by loved ones at the end of this book, she's done a lot of growing. I have truly enjoyed chronicling her journey.

Gabby has been quite a force to deal with. Countless times, I wanted stories to go one way, but Gabby had her own ideas. I finally just let her lead me. I know it was actually God leading, but I like to think Gabby had some hand in it, too. She sure is stubborn, but I love her.

I hope you have enjoyed this series as much as I have enjoyed writing it. For now, Gabby's story has come to an end, although I may do a bonus book in the future if inspiration leads me to it. I have an idea for a book, but I have other projects I need to work on. I've learned when it comes to this series to never say never. Gabby might have more she wants to do.

A special thank you to Carlie Frech, Belinda Martin and Katie Hoffman for being my beta reader team and

listening to all my angst and concerns and offering feedback. A huge thank you, as always, to my husband, Kevin. I truly could not do this without him. We spend hours talking over plot points and places where I'm stuck. He is wonderful at storytelling and helps me come up with some of the wilder ideas. (It was his idea to have Lucas flat line, so you can thank him for that) Discussing the book with him always gets me back on track and my creativity flowing again.

I can not thank you enough for reading all seven books in this series. I have said many times that I have the best readers in the world and I do. If this series is your first taste of my work, you may love some of my other books. I would recommend "How Murder Saved My Life" as well as "Water for Murder."

If you like creepy thrillers, then the Maddison, Indiana series is a must read. Start with "Marked by Darkness" and hold on for a wild ride.

Please follow me at my fan club on Facebook and by signing up for my newsletter. Both are interesting and entertaining. Thanks for reading!

God Bless,
Dawn Merriman

www.DawnMerriman.com